The Last Aeon
Terran Armor Corps Book 5

Richard Fox

Copyright © 2018 Richard Fox

All rights reserved.

ISBN: 1724216228
ISBN-13: 978-1724216229

Prologue

An alabaster tree levitated over a box filled with pitch-black soil. The bottom of the trunk was a jagged edge, as though it had been ripped from its roots and plunked onto the pedestal. Long branches arced over the atrium, glowing with light that diffused through the chamber.

Stacey Ibarra walked around the tree, staring up at the gossamer-thin leaves that glinted with light blue as they flexed in an unfelt breeze. She touched her chin and stepped from side to side, changing her angle on the strange tree. Her fingers rubbed together and she reached for a leaf.

"I wouldn't do that if I were you," Pa'lon said as he walked up behind her.

Stacey snatched her hand back and smiled at the Dotari ambassador.

"Just trying to see if it's real or not," she said. "What do the Qa'Resh call these? And how can it survive if it isn't even planted?" Stacey brushed a strand of hair behind an ear and bent over to look into the gap between the tree and the soil.

"The Qa'Resh don't give names to things," Pa'lon said. He looked like a man in his early fifties with salt-and-pepper black hair and a respectable beard, but Stacey knew he was an alien. Every species represented on Bastion had a single ambassador, but the space station kept up a hologram around each individual, matching them to the race of whoever looked upon them. Stacey had wondered what she looked like as a Dotari to Pa'lon, but neither he nor the station's control AI would answer.

"They aren't much for interior design either." She pointed down a hallway with a slightly arched ceiling lit from strips running a few feet above eye level. An oblong window offered a view to a gas-giant planet.

"Over five hundred ambassadors are here," Pa'lon said. "You think they could agree on how to dress the windows?"

"I never thought of that." Stacey frowned.

"You're new here," he said, motioning her forward. "Come. I'm to escort you to the Silent Quarter."

"She's ready?" Stacey's brow perked up. "Grandfather's been asking about Trinia since I first came here. Said he hasn't spoken with her in—"

Pa'lon looked up at the ceiling and shook his head while tapping an ear.

"What's wrong?" Stacey asked.

"Station intervention," said a monotone voice coming from the ceiling. "Uncleared discussion area."

"I'm not privy to the details," Pa'lon said. "The AI does that from time to time. Come with me."

He turned and walked down the hallway, hands clasped behind his back.

Stacey hurried and fell in next to him. She watched Pa'lon closely, searching for any break or error in the hologram, but if there was any way to glimpse the Dotari underneath the holo, she couldn't find it.

The temptation to reach out and feel the loose tendrils on

his head was real, but one of the first lessons she learned about Bastion was most explicit. No touching.

"Why's it called the Silent Quarter?" she asked.

Pa'lon glanced at her and stopped in front of an elevator. He waved a palm across a panel and a green light blinked.

"It is fitting," he said. "Bastion has been the home of the Alliance for several thousand years. During that time some member races have…fallen away. Others were overtaken by the Xaros. Most ambassadors choose to return to their home world when that happens. Some stay on as mentors and tech experts, but they have no voting rights."

"Wait, Trinia is—"

The elevator doors opened and Stacey took a step back. The elevator walls were clear, and a hull door opening into vacuum brought back her naval training. A hand slapped against her hip, searching for a phantom helmet and air supply. The smear of the Milky Way led into the gas giant, the binary stars of the system's primaries blazing above the galaxy's backbone.

"Get used to this." Pa'lon stepped into the elevator and Stacey took a tentative step onto a wide disk.

"Old habits," she said, looking back and around the hull of the massive space station.

Steel-blue metal stretched out for miles and two pillars tipped with minarets marked the edge. She'd tried to work out the station's size several times, but each time she tried to estimate the circumference her math was wildly different—almost like the station changed itself to keep her from learning too much. And she was certain the size and color of the system's primaries had changed since her arrival less than a week ago.

She reached out and touched an invisible wall, and the elevator moved along the hull without any sense of inertia. She widened her stance and crouched slightly.

Pa'lon laughed. "The exterior lines are always a treat," he said.

"Not if I throw up on you." Stacey brushed her hands over her jumpsuit. Fashion had no meaning when everyone else saw you as a hologram of their own species. She'd opted to dress casual. "I was never one for wild rides like this. You've been to the Silent Quarter before?"

"My mentor spent some time there," Pa'lon said.

"Perhaps you can introduce me? I'm sure he has some funny stories about you that will make me feel less awkward everywhere I go," she said.

"He's…no longer here."

"Oh…I'm an idiot, aren't I? A real diplomat would know better than to say something like that. Why *I'm* on Bastion instead of someone trained to keep their foot out of their mouth is still a mystery to me. I know, Grandfather—babbling. Now I'm babbling."

A door opened against the hull and Stacey jumped back. A narrow hallway led to a small opening and another door.

"This takes some getting used to," Pa'lon said as he held up a hand for Stacey to exit first.

She rushed out, relieved when her feet touched the solid, comforting floor. At the end of the hallway was a small vestibule and a bench.

Pa'lon hesitated in the elevator.

"What's wrong?" she asked.

"I…I thought I could wait for you, but I don't want to go in there," he said. "Memories and implications." He looked up and continued to speak, but Stacey couldn't hear what he was saying. The elevator doors slid shut.

"OK then," Stacey said. "Now what?" She waved a palm over a sensor and nothing happened.

A moment later, the doors opened and a caretaker droid stood before her. Its limbs were pipes as thick as a finger and its face a shovel with a screen mimicking human features.

"Chuck? Haven't seen you since I first arrived," she said.

"Designations are irrelevant," the droid said. "Follow me and do not speak to the other residents."

The shovel face twisted around and the droid led her through a circular room with rows of crystalline trees radiating out from a Qa'Resh probe in the center. The probe was a sliver of glass, emanating gentle light.

Ambassadors sat on benches around the room, some conversing with each other, more than one sitting quietly and staring into the probe. Stacey passed by a disheveled woman who was wiping tears from her eyes. Stacey smiled and gave her a small wave, but the woman didn't acknowledge her.

"Why is there a probe here?" she asked the droid.

"For the dissociated to return home."

"But…aren't they all—"

"It will be their final translation from Bastion. Your appointment." The droid stopped at a set of very tall double doors and one half slid back into the wall. The room beyond was completely dark.

"Did they not pay the power bill?" Stacey asked, looking over the threshold. Not even the ambient light from the chamber cast into the other room.

"Privacy screens are in effect. You are scheduled to return to Earth in the next four hours. Hurry," the droid said.

"Busy busy," she said as she touched a foot onto the dark floor and stepped inside. The room snapped into existence, a laboratory filled with holo stations of spinning DNA strands and men and women standing with their limbs locked in a Vitruvian pose. The stations were all much too large, and the edge of a table she could see was just below her head level.

"What do I—" She turned around, but the door was gone. "No way this can go wrong."

Stacey went into the room and saw that screens on the lab

stations displayed swirling circles of alien text. On the table was a book the size of her torso, with another of the moving circles on the spine. Stacy licked her lips at the thought of touching something so tactile. An actual alien artifact, one without the connection to the genocidal Xaros, was a dream come true for her. The Qa'Resh and other ambassadors hadn't offered her anything like this.

Heavy footsteps vibrated through the floor and she whirled around.

A giant approached: a Nordic-looking woman, ten feet tall, her hair done in intricate braids around the crown of her head. She wore a copper-colored robe that swished around her legs.

Stacey retreated a step and whacked the back of her head against the table edge.

"I'm going to save the human race," the alien said. "And to do that we must destroy everything you believe about your future."

Chapter 1

Stacey watched frost creep out across an armrest of a captain's chair from beneath the touch of her silver fingers. Lifting her arm, she looked across the *Warsaw's* bridge. The layout was much as she remembered from her time aboard the *Breitenfeld*. Her Naval career had been brief as fate had another calling for her.

Navarre, shrouded by clouds the color of old steal, turned in the distance through the forward windows. Echoes of battle commands, whispers of fear between crew stations all harkened back to a very different time in her past.

She looked over a blown-out door, scraped the edge of her foot against a bloodstain and went to the astrogation station. The spot was as she remembered, though the controls had been modified in the nearly twenty years since her brief service on the ship.

She touched the headrest and leaned forward, catching her reflection on a screen. The young woman she'd once been was gone, replaced with a motionless mask on a metal body, a silver mannequin given locomotion with an echo of her true features.

Stacey ripped away the headrest and tossed it aside.

"Admiral Makarov?" she asked.

To the rear of the captain's chair, a woman in her mid-twenties with abyss black hair and alabaster skin stepped forward.

"My Lady?" the admiral asked.

"How long until your ship is ready to fight again?"

"Nineteen hours. The damage we took evacuating Pasaia is nearly repaired. The crew replacements are going through their final drills now," she said.

"Every life lost is a tragedy," Stacey said. "This ship reminds me of another, the *Breitenfeld*, the ship of miracles, where Earth launched the first missions of the Ember War and brought the final battle to the Xaros Masters. She'll be ours soon. As she should be. The Terran Union abandoned the mantle of leadership when they signed the Hale Treaty and turned away from protecting our future."

"Pasaia was the last of our colonies in the galaxy with a legacy Crucible," Marshall Davoust said. "What of our other worlds?"

"It was a mistake to settle systems known to New Bastion before our relationship with the rest of the galaxy was set," Stacey said. "I didn't think the Terran Union or the aliens would turn on us as hard as they did on Balmaseda…but our colonies in nearby stars are all within the gate network we built for ourselves. Navarre is the only link to them. We lose this system and the rest are at risk, until then they are safe. Continue the fortifications. Besides, if we were to evacuate some of the…special populations, the trauma would be severe."

"We do not question your vision." Davoust said. "The war will be won. The Ibarra Nation will survive, even if we must secure that right at the barrel of a gun."

"We can pay that price in blood, or we can win with one swift stroke," Stacey said. "And to save our lives we need the last Aeon…and we need the *Breitenfeld*. I trust Admiral Makarov to retrieve the first asset."

"You'll not accompany the mission to Ouranos?" Makarov asked.

"I will be there in spirit," Stacey replied. "Make ready. And as Admiral Valdar would say…*Gott Mit Uns*."

****

Roland intoned the last of a prayer and raised his eyes from the sword planted point-down in the floor. Candlelight flickered off a statue of St. Kallen in her wheelchair. He'd seen her depicted in other ways since he returned to Navarre: an apparition walking the battlefield with a nimbus of light around her head; busts of her with hair in a long braid and draped over a shoulder, leaving her skull plugs exposed. Small shrines of her in her wheelchair seemed to be tucked into every common area and office he'd been to.

He rose to his feet and sheathed his sword, then lit a pair of candles. The silence of the empty chapel was almost reverent, though he was used to attending services with many others at the same time. Today was different.

"Thomas Shaw. Catherine Shaw."

He turned around and froze. There was another person in the pews, genuflecting on the kneelers. Roland saw the top of a head of pitch-black hair.

Admiral Makarov crossed herself and looked up at Roland. Despite her high rank, she was nearly the same age as Roland. She'd been brought forth from the procedural crèches with the knowledge and experience of a senior commander, but a younger body to keep her on active duty longer.

"Ma'am," Roland said, nodding to her.

"We've the chapel all to ourselves. You can call me Ivana out of earshot of the crew," she said.

"I've never called a flag officer by their first name before," Roland half-smiled.

"The Lady's Armor stand apart from my chain of command." She went to the statue and looked up at the saint. "You always observe the anniversary of the Lost 8th?"

"My mother wasn't big on church," Roland said, "but we always went to pay our respects on the day the *Midway* returned from the void and we knew father was lost. I've found more religion since then."

"It would be easy to turn this into a time for mourning." She lit a candle. "Admiral Yulia Makarov. The Lost 8th was sent to the void to slow down the Xaros coming from Barnard's Star. From the logs recovered on the *Midway*, my mother could have jumped back to Earth once they encountered Abaddon and all the Xaros inside that dwarf planet."

"Getting spooked and running home wasn't my father's style."

"Nor my mother's. They fought and managed to slow down the Xaros. Bought Earth several more years to prepare, just enough time to make the difference between victory and defeat. We light a candle for the dead who won a victory, not who died in vain," Makarov said.

"I wonder…" Roland shifted uncomfortably. He knew the Makarov standing next to him was a procedural, possessing false memories of her deceased "mother," but Ivana Makarov knew what she was. "I wonder if this is what they would have wanted for us."

"What parent wants their child to fight a war? 'I must study politics and war that my sons may have liberty to study mathematics and philosophy,'" she said.

"John Adams." Roland touched a pocket, then removed a small plastic box with a bit of old-style admiral insignia on it. "You did ask for this back."

"You did return from battle as you promised." Makarov brushed her fingers against his as she took her favor from him. "But, you're assigned to my *Warsaw* for this next mission."

She nudged his arm and they walked out of the chapel into a passageway humming with the sound of sailors working around the corner.

"A mission I don't know much about," Roland muttered.

"You may not be in my chain of command, but I must respect yours to deliver your orders as they see fit." Makarov swiped a hand over her screen and dozens of alert messages scrolled past. She sighed.

"I haven't had the chance to look around Navarre," Roland said. "Are there restaurants? Or theaters or—"

"Nothing like that," Makarov said. "All efforts are going toward the war…though I do have my own personal mess and can invite whoever I like to it. After this mission?" She raised an eyebrow.

"I'll accept your invitation as another lady's favor," Roland said.

"Then may the Saint be with you." Makarov glanced at a blinking alert message. "And with my quartermaster in about three minutes, when I figure out why we don't have any rail cannon shells for the forward battery."

She looked up and down the passageway, then gave Roland's hand a quick squeeze before she left.

Chapter 2

A mule ramp lowered with a hiss of hydraulics and cold, dry air flooded the transport. Chief Santos felt the bite against his bare skin from where he stood at the fore of the compartment. The many Rangers packed tight in there with him didn't seem to mind.

The hangar beyond opened up to a magnificent sunset; the system's two primaries—a large yellow and smaller white star—hung just over the horizon. Long shadows stretched from slate-colored mountain peaks and cut across a valley leading to the base of the mountain Santos had just landed inside.

A sergeant in gray-scale fatigues and a black beret stomped up the ramp, his breath fogging in the air as he looked across the personnel crammed into the Mule. His eyes carried the faraway quality of one that spent too much time in combat.

"Rangers! Welcome to Umbra. Welcome to the fight. Police your gear and follow me." He half turned and swung an arm forward.

The soldiers grunted and cursed as they tried to untangle themselves and their packs from each other, hurrying after the sergeant, each departure lessening the pressure on Santos and the rest.

A Ranger swung her pack onto her shoulders. "Good luck," she said to him and tapped her fist to her heart in a salute.

Santos managed a nod and a half smile. Acknowledging Saint Kallen was strictly forbidden these days, especially after what happened on Mars.

"Thanks," he said. "Stay safe out there."

"Like that'll happen," she muttered and hurried out of the Mule.

He picked up his rucksack, decidedly less heavy than the gear the Rangers were carrying, and walked to the edge of the ramp. The hangar was alive with activity as techs loaded munitions onto a pair of Eagles, both sporting dents and scorch marks from battle damage. Troops moved about in loose formations to exits.

Loaders in powered exoskeletons moved crates to waiting hover sleds. The shouting of sergeants and chief petty officers turned what looked like chaos into a ballet of moving pieces dancing on the edge of chaos.

"Chief Santos?" A man in dirty overalls and with dark hair mostly run through with gray looked up at him from one side of the ramp.

"That's me," he said. "How'd you know?"

The tech tapped the back of his skull, indicating Santos's plugs. "You don't blend, sir," he said. "Master Sergeant Henrique. I'm your lance technician chief. Captain Gideon sent me to pick you up."

Santos nodded and went down the ramp. As a junior Armor soldier, he had no illusions about his importance, but he thought at least one of his lance mates would have come to pick him up, not a suit tech.

"Where is the captain?" Santos asked as he followed Henrique through the busy hangar.

"He dismounted and went to some powwow with the brass," Henrique said. "Captain gave the Kesaht a bloody nose in the valley. He'd still be out there, but it's almost sundown."

"How does that matter?" Santos frowned and looked to the horizon and the suns nestled within layers of golden bands.

"They didn't tell you about Umbra?" Henrique asked.

"I didn't get much. Personnel showed up, handed a bunch of us orders, and told us to get through the Mars Crucible ASAP. Kind of a surprise. Graduation wasn't for another two months." Santos shrugged the shoulder holding the rucksack, alleviating the bite of the strap somewhat.

"You didn't finish training?" Henrique did a double take.

"Well, that last field op is sort of a waste of time, so I've heard. I'm ready. Where's my suit?" He flashed a very wide—and very fake—smile.

"*Cagnar nas callas*," Henrique muttered in Portuguese. "The Corps cut off its nose to spite its own face."

"Sorry, what?"

"Nothing, sir. Welcome to the Iron Dragoons. You're filling some awfully big boots. Just don't want you to end up like the last guy."

Henrique hefted Santos's pack off his back and tossed it into the rear of a hover cart. As the cart took off around the corner, the Armor soldier looked back for a last glimpse of the sunset.

****

Santos bounded up the corrugated metal steps leading to a catwalk spanning across a makeshift cemetery—not one for the departed, but for Armor suits standing inside maintenance bays shaped like coffins missing their lids.

He noted blaster score marks on the breastplate of one, the half-blackened unit patch of the Iron Dragoons and bubbled paint from a Kesaht blast. When he passed a factory-fresh suit, the smell of grease and the glint of new optics made him smile.

An Armor soldier was a few suits away, facing away from Santos, but the plugs on the back of his head marked him out as one of Mars' champions.

With a stomp of his foot, Santos came to a stop and rendered a perfect salute.

"Warrant Officer 1 Mateo Santos reporting for duty, sir!"

The other Armor turned around, snapping straight a metal

prosthetic hand. Aignar clumsily returned the salute.

Santos's eyes widened as he looked at Aignar's robotic hands and the speaker in his throat, but he regained his military bearing a moment later.

"Jonas Aignar. They said we had a replacement inbound. Didn't think you'd be so…squeaky." The man's mouth and jaw didn't move; all his words came from his throat speaker.

"I'm fully rated," Santos said. "Top of my class in marksmanship and tactics. Sure, we didn't get our final evaluations, but—"

"Let me see your ORB." Aignar's salute hand bent into a fist.

Santos removed a slate from his pocket and swiped it on. His Officer Record Brief, a chronological list of his entire military career, training and assignments, was already loaded up.

Aignar's eyebrows perked up.

"Jesus, kid. You're still pissing Martian water. No prior service. You assessed straight to Knox and then Mars." Aignar looked up from the slate and shook his head.

"Is that…bad? Plenty of Armor come through that way."

"They don't go through and miss the last maneuver exercise before going downrange. This ain't training, kid. No place to dip your toe in and test the water. You're in the deep end with the sharks. Kesaht out there aren't fooling around."

"I'm ready," Santos said, swallowing hard.

"Sure you are." Aignar handed the slate back to the junior soldier. He banged a metal wrist against the railing and got Henrique's attention on the ground level. "Cherry needs to plug in," he shouted down.

"It's an honor to be with this lance," Santos said. "I heard all about the fight on Barada, Balmaseda, and even—"

"Let me stop you right there, kid. The Iron Dragoons go back a long way, to old horse cavalry in the American army. Recent past has been a bit…checkered. You know about the Templar?"

"They defected to the Ibarra Nation. Some sort of jailbreak on Mars? I was doing gunnery quals on Titan when all that went down. Sounded like a real mess. Ibarran spies. Lots of naissance checks for the support crew. I've got my plugs, so there shouldn't be any doubt I'm loyal to the Union. I'm no proccie the Ibarras could have tinkered with."

"Being true born's no guarantee," Aignar said. "You keep to Saint Kallen?"

"I was raised original Catholic," Santos said. "I know what Kallen did, but I don't believe in her that way."

"One less thing to worry about. You know whose spot you're filling?"

"Sure don't. Orders said Iron Dragoons on Umbra." He shrugged.

"You're either out of the loop or General Laran's done a great job of blotting out his name from the records. You seen that vid from Balmaseda, the Black Knight on the bridge holding off Sanheel?"

"A couple hundred times. That Armor's a legend for how he…" Santos frowned. "Wait…if he…oh. Oh!" He twisted around and stared at the new suit of Armor. "Wait. Really? Seriously?"

"Gideon's going to love you. I can feel it." Aignar raised a shoulder and scratched the side of his face against his coveralls. His jaw was off-kilter for a half second until he knocked it back into place with a tap of his metal fist.

"His name is Roland Shaw. He's a traitor and a coward,"

Aignar said. "He's gone from the Terran Union and the Corps. Never speak of him. Don't ask the captain about him. He's the enemy now. If we ever cross paths with him, you put him down like you would any Kesaht. Understand?"

"We're going to fight Ibarrans?" Santos asked.

"Not here. Not unless they show up looking for a scrap. Bastards here are giving us enough trouble for the system. But there's a reckoning coming for the Ibarrans. All of them," Aignar said.

"The Terran Union is humanity," Santos said. "My father was there—I mean, he fought in the Ember War. The Ibarrans are targets. All of them. Roger that."

"You're the fourth Iron Dragoon. You'll earn your spurs with us or die trying," Aignar said.

"I am Armor," Santos said, his eyes set firm. He looked down the line of suits in the cemetery. "Who's the third?"

"Cha'ril. She's on maternity leave," Aignar said.

"What? How did that happen?"

"She's Dotari, but I've heard the mechanics are pretty similar."

"No. I mean, why—but if she's…They never mentioned stuff like this in training."

"Welcome to the 'real' army. Training's over with. Enemy's plenty real. Now let's get you plugged in. Captain will be back soon and we're not going to be here much longer, not with nightfall coming."

Chapter 3

Cha'ril groaned and leaned forward. Man'fred Vo caught her and sprinkled water over her hair quills. Vapor rose from them as she began panting.

"You're doing great!" Man'fred Vo said as he raised a spoon up to her beak. "Ice chips?"

Cha'ril slapped the spoon away and snapped at his face.

"The apex is free," a nurse said from the other side of the nest.

"It's finally out?" Cha'ril squeaked.

"It's beautiful." Man'fred Vo hugged her tight and helped her roll over.

The egg lay on a padded tray, the shell white and speckled with deep-blue spots. A Dotari nurse wiped it clean as another ran a sensor wand over the top. The egg was oval-shaped, almost as long as her forearm.

"Everything is viable," the nurse said. "Congratulations."

"The spots...my mother said my sisters had the same pattern," Man'fred Vo said and gave Cha'ril's shoulder a squeeze.

"I hate you. Oh, how I hate you right now," she said.

"They all say that." The nurse let out a staccato hiss of a laugh.

Cha'ril propped herself up and shifted against the edge of the nest bed. She stared hard at the egg, her fingers opening and closing.

"You wish to hold it?" the nurse asked.

"I am...I am of the warrior list," she said. "It's bad luck. Isn't it?" She looked up at Man'fred Vo, her eyes pleading.

"I am on the same list," he said. "We know the stories. The Tragedy of Gol-rin. Uella's Lonely Nest."

"Then I will take this to the incubation ward," the nurse said. "Transport back to the home world is ready. You've arranged for a ward?"

"Our mothers," Cha'ril said. "But we want the incubation

slowed. Long enough for our service terms to end."

"Easily done." The nurse put a palm to the egg. "The first Dotari laid on Mars. Congratulations."

The nurse pushed the cart away and Cha'ril lurched forward, but Man'fred Vo pulled her back.

"We agreed," he said.

"Your blood isn't hot with maternal instincts like mine," she said, slumping forward.

"You are…" he pushed her quills to one side to see her skull plugs, "you are special, my star. The Armor would let you leave?"

"I've read the mutual defense treaty a dozen times," she said. "The humans insisted on a clause allowing Dotari mothers to end their service in the event of pregnancy. Seems human females experience worse labor than us." She scooted to the edge of the nest and got to her feet carefully.

"Then you could take it," Man'fred Vo said. "Go back to the home world with our egg until it—"

"Would you leave your squadron now?"

Man'fred Vo let out a low trill.

"Your father is a great pilot. A renowned war hero. Your

duty is not done to the Dotari or our alliance with Earth. Neither is mine. I am Armor…my lance needs me."

"Your lance is a dirty nest," he said. "The human Armor just went through a civil war, one that isn't over. Earth promised they'd keep Dotari out of the conflict with the Ibarrans, but you're in a joint lance. You could end up fighting that…that Roland. That one our *ushulra* will never speak of."

"I should just abandon the humans when they need every Armor they can throw into the fight?"

"You don't owe them—"

"*We* owe them, Man'fred Vo. I'm alive because a Strike Marine sniper chose to save my mother and me when I was a baby in her arms. Marines bled and died for that decision. *We* live because the *Breitenfeld* saved us on Takeni. How can I turn my back on them now?"

"Then transfer to a Dotari Armor battalion. Don't risk getting in the middle of their vendettas."

Cha'ril winced as her hip bones popped.

"We're in the war against the Kesaht with Earth—the rest of the Vishrakath's alliance too if they attack our ships," she said.

"There's no safe place for me. Or you. Is that what this is about?"

"After the Ibarrans almost killed me during their escape." His quills rustled with annoyance. "Flying fighters gives one a sense of invincibility. When an explosion tears that fighter apart and an ejection seat saves your life…It made me think."

"Armor is not a safe assignment. Even in a Dotari battalion," she said, pulling a robe over her shoulders.

"I want us *both* to be there when our egg hatches…but at least one must be there," he said. "For the egg. For our child."

"So one of us must leave the fight now…or we both survive the war."

"If you were a pilot, I could protect you in the air—"

"And if you were Armor, we'd fight shoulder to shoulder. I am Armor. I must fight."

"I cannot leave my wing."

"Then…"

"I swear," he said, swinging his legs over the nest and folding her hands into his, "I will be there when our baby reaches into the light."

"We can promise all we want. The war carries its own fate

for us. It's not that I doubt you, my joined, but I did think you died during the Ibarrans' escape." She slapped him on the shoulder.

"Then if one of us is lost?"

"The other leaves the war. Returns to the home world and is a parent to our child."

"Agreed," Man'fred Vo said. "This…this is not a conversation I ever thought I'd have with my joined."

"Then you shouldn't have fought so hard for my hand!" She gave him a playful punch on the shoulder.

"It was love at first sight. I regret nothing."

"It was my pheromones." She clicked her beak.

"No. It wasn't," he said as he wrapped his arms around her shoulders and pulled her close.

Chapter 4

The briefing room aboard the *Warsaw* was little different from other Terran Union capital ships: semicircular rows radiating away from a small stage and holo tank. Ship's officers and a pair of Armor from another lance mingled about the room. Roland stood next to Morrigan as she leaned against a row of seats, arms and legs crossed.

"Its bloody shite is what it is," said the Irish Armor.

"You've never been on full commo lockdown before?" Roland asked. "Happens all the time in my…my old unit." He cleared his throat nervously. His defection from the Terran Union to the Ibarra Nation was sealed after he broke out of a Martian prison and fought Union Armor to rescue Lady Ibarra from a Qa'Resh facility. Despite this, he still felt out of place amongst those he now fought beside.

"Wasn't necessary before we brought Earth's Templar and a few hundred…ach, what're we calling them? Have to be polite all of a sudden."

"Sleeper agents," Roland said. The soldiers, sailors and Marines who had once been loyal to Earth had become full-on Ibarrans after the rescue team activated dormant commands in some of his fellow prisoners. Seeing them change so quickly and easily had been a little hard for Roland to accept.

"Now we have to get our mission orders just before we step off," Morrigan said. "No time for rehearsals. No time to hit the range and shoot up proper targets."

"If you lived in a constant state of preparedness, there would be no need to worry," said one of the pair of Armor soldiers as the two came over. Both were Asian men with shaved heads, their skull plugs glinting in the light.

"If I want crap from you, Umezu, I'll squeeze your head," Morrigan said.

"We have our duty," said the other Armor, Araki by his name tape, "and that is all we must concern ourselves with."

"I can't tell if the Nisei lance are fatalists or posers," Morrigan said.

"Discipline equals freedom, Morrigan," Umezu said. "Send us through a drop pod to scout a planet? We are ready. Assault Phoenix and bring the Union to its knees? Give us a landing zone."

Morrigan made a dismissive noise and rolled her eyes.

"How is the Black Knight adjusting to the Nation?" Araki asked Roland.

"I had the nickel tour before the legionnaires and the *Warsaw* got me off Mars," Roland said. "The hardest thing is the Basque language, though everyone switches to English when they realize…" he added, tapping his skull plugs.

"Basque." Umezu shivered. "Almost no mutual intelligibility with English or the old Atlantic Union languages. It's like when my uncle tried to teach me Japanese."

"Nisei…" Roland looked at their lance insignia on the men's arms, a torch held up on a blue field.

"Our parents were refugees," Araki said. "Fled Chinese occupation to America. There was a regiment that fought in the Second World War made up of second-generation Japanese. It fit for our lance, though we weren't recruited out of an internment camp like the original Nisei regiment."

"Sounds like someone I know." Morrigan jabbed an elbow into Roland's ribs.

Nicodemus entered the briefing room, walking with a slight limp. His complexion was ashen.

"You look like ass," Morrigan said. "Not good ass either."

"I'm fine," said the other Templar. "Full medical scan cleared me for duty."

"You got banged on Nunavik," she said. "If you come that close to redlining, you're supposed to be taken off the line to recover."

"Cleared for duty," Nicodemus said. "Just finished a holo with the family…my wife is very close to her due date. I arranged for more household droids, but that's not what she wants from me."

"No way to win this one," Morrigan said.

"We win whatever fight we're being sent to and come home fast," Nicodemus said. "Though the baby will come when the baby will come. They're selfish that way."

Roland thought back to Cha'ril, who he last heard was expecting. When Aignar shared that news with him, they were the last kind words his former lance mate ever said to him.

A sergeant major, part of the Ibarran Armor's staff, came into the room and stomped a foot as he braced himself against the wall next to the door.

"Room, atten-shun!"

Roland clicked his heels together and brought his shoulders back slightly, locking hands against the seam of his trousers.

Colonel Martel and General Hurson went to the stage. The general spoke quietly to Martel for a moment then left.

"Be seated," Martel said as the lights dimmed and a holo wall came to life behind him. "Armor, we have a critical mission. Lances Templar and Nisei will accompany an…envoy to Ouranos, a world on the spinward side of the Perseus arm."

A map of the galaxy came up, along with an overlay of areas claimed by the Milky Way's species. The Terran Union had patches of control across the galaxy, along with a wide berth around Earth. Ouranos was far from Earth space, just on the edge of a wide swath of magenta.

"Who are the Cyrgal?" Roland wondered out loud. He shut up as Martel looked at him.

"Ouranos is a protectorate world," Martel said. "While Bastion was the home to the old Alliance, a number of ambassadors' species went nearly extinct, with only the ambassador surviving. Some of those survivors escaped Bastion's destruction and made it home. New Bastion placed those worlds in a protectorate status, and there are only a half dozen across the galaxy. The Terran Union protects the Karigole, for those Ember War historians."

The holo zoomed in on Ouranos, a blue and green world that could have been Earth's cousin. A dashed outline of a humanoid form came up next to the planet and dashed lines traced from the form's head and feet to a point just off the coast.

"The last Aeon should be here," Martel said. "Lady Ibarra has tasked us with retrieving the Aeon and returning her to Navarre. I'll now turn this briefing over to the envoy."

Roland felt a chill breeze as a man in a legionnaire uniform with no insignia and full face helmet walked onto the stage. The man didn't move with the confidence or alertness of a legionnaire…this man had a swagger to him.

"Oh no," Roland said.

Marc Ibarra removed his helmet and Nicodemus slammed a fist against his seat.

"Hello, hello!" Marc handed the helmet toward Martel, who didn't take it. "Some old faces out there in the crowd, I see. Nicodemus! Bet you never thought I'd get out of that cell after you arrested me! And there's my boy!" He wagged a finger at Roland and Roland wished he could melt into the back of his chair and disappear.

"Did you two get matching prison tats?" Morrigan whispered to Roland and he grumbled a nonresponse.

"We're off to meet my old pen pal, an Aeon by the name of Trinia," Ibarra said. "But I'm a little ahead of myself. When a Qa'Resh probe first contacted me on Earth, the plan to use a time skip on a fleet and retake Earth and the incomplete Crucible was drawn up. Now, I could only save a small fraction of Earth's population, and that wasn't going to be enough to stop the Xaros when they came back. You all lived through that bit.

"The Qa'Resh had an idea to repopulate the Earth and that's

where Trinia came in. She is a biologist—one with thousands of years of experience—and I was able to feed her enough data through the Qa'Resh probe back to Bastion where her lab was. It took several decades of work, but she broke the code on how to grow an adult human in nine days and put a trained mind into that body. She was the mind behind the procedurals. Granted, I did all the hard work on Earth gathering data and—"

"What do we need a biologist for?" Nicodemus asked.

"We don't need a *biologist*, per se." Marc touched a lectern and frost spread out across the front. "We need someone with a deeper understanding of Qa'Resh technology. The Qa'Resh worked in the smallest possible increments. All about quantum states and designations. What's fascinating about that mindset is that once you've mastered the base of their language, you know it all. For instance, I don't speak French, but if you put a line of that language on the screen, I can read it aloud. I won't know if I asked what's for dinner or just propositioned your cat, but the words will come out. With Qa'Resh, if you can read it, you understand it. All of it. You grok."

Roland frowned at Morrigan, who shrugged her shoulders.

"And what do we need this super reader for?" Marc pulled his hand away with a snap of ice and brushed frost out of his palm. "I'm glad you asked. Slide." He said the last word to Martel.

The colonel stepped away from the lectern.

"Fine, fine." Marc reached over and swiped a hand over a screen hidden in the stand. A grainy image of a ship floating in space appeared on the holo wall. The alien vessel resembled a conch shell, with long spines tipped with silver metal and a white marble hull. An Ibarran carrier appeared next to the ship for scale; the alien ship was easily five times larger.

"We call it the Ark," Marc said. "It is the single-greatest piece of Qa'Resh technology left over after their exit off this plane of existence. If we can seize control of this, the balance of power will forever change in the galaxy. Jump-engine technology. Energy weapons we saw used during the last battle with the Xaros that could annihilate fleets in an instant."

"Where is it?" Morrigan asked.

"Stac—Lady Ibarra knows where it is," Marc said. "And…she's not shared that with me. Or anyone else. But she also knows her comprehension of Qa'Resh technology isn't enough to fully utilize this ship. The Ark isn't of much use to us if all we can do is turn the lights on and off."

"Why will this Aeon help us?" Kataro, one of the Niseai, asked.

"I have something to offer her," Marc said, "something no one else in the galaxy has. You let me worry about that part, yeah?"

"You sure she's alive?" Nicodemus said. "The Xaros destroyed Bastion a long time ago."

"Aeon are naturally long-lived," Marc said. "And two years ago a Kroar raiding force arrived in system. None of the Kroar survived. The Cyrgal reported the incident and that the Aeon was unharmed to New Bastion."

"You think these Cyrgal will be happy to see us?" Nicodemus asked.

Marc raised his hands and rotated them from side to side.

"Tough to say. Tough to say," he said. The image on the holo wall changed to a bipedal alien with a hairless, leonine head. A simple tunic covered the torso and cloth wrapped around the legs and arms—one of the two sets of arms. The bottom pair were mechanical and had the same four fingers as the true hands.

"Cyrgal are a bit of an enigma," Marc said. "Their territory spanned several star systems and they had a population in the hundreds of billions *before* the Qa'Resh contacted them. They've been very slow to expand since the end of the war, but they take their duty of protecting Ouranous very seriously. Their culture and politics are fractious, to say the least. Clans and extended tribes are constantly in a state of low-level conflict with each other. Trying to get them to agree on anything is almost impossible, but there are two exceptions: when threatened, they will work together quite handily, and they all take certain aspects of their religion as a matter of life and death.

"The Aeon—oddly enough—fits into their belief pantheon as some sort of creator figure. So long as we don't come in guns blazing, we should have enough time to convince Trinia to leave with us before things get too hairy," Marc said.

"The Cyrgal are effectively neutral in the Vishrakath-led war against Earth and our Nation," Martel said. "Lady Ibarra would prefer we avoid drawing them into the conflict, but securing the Aeon is our number-one priority."

"They're just going to let us waltz up to this god figure and skip away with her?" Morrigan asked.

"I can be very convincing," Marc said. "And let me add this. Without Trinia, we would have lost the Ember War. Period. Humanity would be extinct. We would not have survived the second Xaros attack without the procedural technology, and without that win, we would have never brought the fight to the Xaros Masters and destroyed them. Bastion would be thinking up another Hail Mary play to survive the Xaros drones' advance without her work and without our spilled blood. So we owe Trinia. We owe her the chance I'm going to give her."

Chapter 5

Roland, in Armor, stood with his lance in a *Warsaw* munition bay. A hundred-foot-long missile with four compartments built into the base of the nosecone radiated steam and heat as massive servo arms lifted a heavy plate off one of the compartments. A frame within could hold an Armor soldier with little room to spare.

"Nothing like a tactical insertion torpedo to make an entrance," Roland said.

"The Cyrgal defend the Ouranos system," Martel said. "Their military is organized around massive capital ships to fend off invasions, not raids. The *Warsaw* won't do a slingshot orbit pass like she did to get us off Mars."

"There's no such thing as a tactical *extraction* torpedo," Roland said. "How are we getting off world?"

"Makarov's keeping that close hold," Nicodemus said.

"She's not let us down before."

"She doesn't trust us?" Roland asked.

"It's not a matter of trust," came from a smaller stairway built for normal-sized crew. Marc Ibarra made his way onto the platform, followed by two of Stacey Ibarra's much larger bodyguards. "It's a matter of loose lips sinking ships."

"Well," Morrigan said, turning her helm to the silver man, "if it isn't the traitor that tried to tell our enemies Navarre's location and the Lady's plans. Come to lecture us on operation security. What a day."

"If Stacey can put things in the past for the greater good," Marc wagged a finger at Nicodemus, "I can get over having my personage being manhandled by a brute like him. You know he slapped that metal mitt of his over my face for hours before he chucked me into a cell? If I had a sense of smell or needed to breathe, I might never have recovered."

"You know how we're getting off Ouranos?" Roland asked.

"Well...not exactly." Marc shrugged. "I can hazard a guess but speculation only introduces doubt into an operation, as does ambiguity, so let's not overthink this. However we're getting off world, the means are so delicate that if Trinia or the Cyrgal get word of it, it won't work."

"This does nothing for my confidence levels," Morrigan said.

"All you've got to do is keep the Cyrgal away with your fearsome reputation and big scary guns while I work my magic on Trinia. Now, a little direction. Ready?" Marc held his hands up and made a rough square like he was looking through a camera. "Give me 'crush your head'! Yes, excellent. Now, how about 'I'll rip your limbs off and beat your friend to death with them'?"

Morrigan stepped toward Marc but Nicodemus stopped her with his arm.

"This'll be a breeze," Marc said. "So, where's my torp?"

"You'll ride with Roland," Martel said.

"He'll what?" Roland asked.

Marc craned his neck up and looked into the open compartment.

"You don't breathe," Martel said. "You don't have internal organs or a blood supply affected by acceleration or high-g maneuvers. We're not even sure how much damage your…body can take. The Terran Union has a few prototype insertion torps for Strike Marines, but recreating that tech for you is a waste of time and resources."

"Gee thanks." Marc put his hands on his hips. "So how do I—"

"The shock frame's been adjusted to accommodate you," Martel said. "Roland won't deploy with a Mouser heavy rifle. I'll carry it for him."

"Why him? Maybe I should go down with the Nisei. They're loading up in the other bay. I'll just—" Marc backed away and one of the bodyguards nudged him in the small of the back with his rifle.

"He's the junior lancer," Martel said. "He always pulls the shortest straw."

"Of all the traditions to carry over from the Terran Armor Corps…" Roland went to the opening and crawled inside, like he was a bullet loading into a breech. Crash frames closed against his legs and shoulders. Were he not used to being inside an armored pod filled with amniosis fluid, the claustrophobia would have been palpable.

"So I just…" Marc hopped up beside the compartment. "A ladder or—unhand me you oaf!"

Nicodemus grabbed Marc around the waist and slid him next to Roland, who put his arm around Marc's shoulder.

The compartment closed over them and bars wedged Marc against Roland's side. Weak red light filled the tight space.

"We will never speak of this," Marc said.

"I always wanted my own little sidekick," Roland said.

"I am over a hundred years old and would be the richest person in human history had Garret not used eminent domain to—"

"I think I'll call you George," Roland said. "I will hug you and squeeze you—"

"Let me out!" Marc wiggled against Roland, but he was held fast. Frost crept over Roland's Armor.

"Pat you and love you and…you know what? It is getting a little weird."

"You think?" Marc stopped struggling. "How do we get out of these things?"

"The torp dumps us out. Sometimes at a velocity that allows me to manage a graceful landing. Sometimes."

"Just don't use me to cushion your fall, you hear me, Roland?"

The torpedo rotated clockwise, bringing around the next compartment for a Templar to load up.

"Roland?"

"I promise nothing."

****

The *Warsaw* materialized out of a wormhole not far from a poorly formed moon; its axis was off, like a giant had gripped the celestial body and twisted it against itself. A squadron of destroyers and frigates followed, forming a cordon around the Ibarran carrier.

A pair of torpedoes shot out the ventral tubes just beneath the internal flight deck and arced around the moon. On the bridge, Admiral Makarov brought her holo tank to life and watched as the local system materialized before her.

"Guns, any activity from the moon?" she asked.

"Negative, ma'am. This moon's surface is unstable, doubt the locals can even keep passive sensors functioning down there," the gunnery officer, Eneko, said.

"They're going to notice the graviton waves from our entrance," the XO, Commander Andere said. "We came in right on top of the Lagrange point...which just shifted out of alignment with the Crucible we did our offset jump through."

"Our intelligence was correct," Makarov said. "The Cyrgal are sloppy. They left a back door for us to slip in through...now we're being hailed. Maybe they're not that clueless."

"Launch the alert fighters?" Andere asked.

"No." Makarov brought the hail up in the holo tank and frowned as there were eight different channels part of one frequency. "Our arrival's riled them up enough. Now we de-escalate."

Makarov opened the hail, and windows with Cyrgal faces formed a row in front of her face. The males were larger and gruff-looking, and most of their faces were similarly lined and scarred to such a degree that Makarov suspected they were of the same age. The females had a thin layer of fur and shawls over their heads with beads and small coins woven into the edge.

"Terran vessel," a male said, "this is protected space. Your arrival here is unauthorized and unwelcome. You will set course for the Crucible at once and—"

"I am Admiral Makarov of the Ibarra Nation vessel *Warsaw*," she said. "We stand apart from the Terran Union. We are here to establish diplomatic relations with you and—"

"Where is the rest of your kindred?" a female asked. "Does this Ibarra Nation insult us with a *xeren*?"

The channel froze but remained open.

"Damn me for not anticipating this." Makarov waved her XO and a legionnaire sentry over. "Take your helmets off and stand on either side of me. Cyrgal are group decision makers. They never send just one of them to do anything. That *xeren* they mentioned—"

"Ibarran?" A Cyrgal male with a cybernetic eye spoke. Only his window was active; the others were still frozen. "You are not *xeren*?"

"There is no concept of this for humans. I am with my executive officer and my-my chief of internal discipline. Decisions are relayed through me and as such—"

"Then our kindred will be represented in full," the cyborg said with a sigh of relief. The other seven windows reactivated. "We are Kul Rui Gassla, confederated with the Forssui aboard the *Concord of Might*. This confederation is bound by blood and immutable."

"Good to know," Makarov said. The brief from the intelligence section had neglected to mention any of what this Cyrgal has just laid out. She muted the channel and turned to Anderre. "Get the intelligence officer up here. Now."

The legionnaire inched away as the XO left, but Makarov grabbed him by the belt and set him on her flank.

"Our instructions to you remain," a female said. "Leave this system immediately."

"By New Bastion decree nineteen," Makarov said, "dated Third Standard Year four hundred and eighty-fifth hour. We are exercising our right to establish contact with the Aeon as laid out in—"

"The Ibarra Nation is not signatory to the accords," said a male with a scar running through his lips. "New Bastion agreements do not apply to you."

"When the Ibarra Nation was founded, we agreed to all treaties the Terran Union ratified. I will forward you the documents if you like." Makarov smiled and the Cyrgal males bared their teeth at her. She wiped the smile away and the males seemed to calm down.

"Consultation," a female said and their pictures froze.

"We did?" the legionnaire asked.

"Of course not," Makarov said. "But I have hundreds of pages of misleading and contradictory documents—in Basque—for them to paw through. We need to stall them while the Armor and Ibarra find the Aeon and convince her to help us."

The Cyrgal came back online.

"*Warsaw*," said the cyborg-eyed alien, "we are unable to verify your claim."

"Well, then I'll transmit everything you'll need."

"Our ambassadors on New Bastion are aware of sanctions against the Ibarra kindred. There is disagreement regarding whether you are in violation of the Hale Treaty. Are any aboard your ships… First Mother's hand this is confusing…"

A female with a deep-blue shawl continued. "Are any of your crew created after—"

"None of your business," Makarov said. "None of mine either. It is against our laws to pry into such matters. Now, I wish to make contact with the Aeon. And your ambassador."

"We must agree to a representative," another female said.

Another group of seven Cyrgal joined the channel and started talking all at once, their language melding into low growls and clicks. More groups filled the channel until the entire holo tank was full of Cyrgal chattering endlessly.

The original group moved to the fore of the holo projection.

"Consultation is required," the cyborg alien said. "Do not threaten the Rui Gassla and you will not be destroyed."

"Acceptable," Makarov said. "As for the Aeon—"

"Ouranos is under the Ban Nala," a female said and spit. The other Cyrgal spat a moment later. "Their business is their own."

"Then how do I—"

The Cyrgal melded back into the giant mass of chattering aliens as Makarov leaned onto the handrails and tried to make sense of the chaos in her holo tank.

"XO, set a slow course to Ouranos," she said. "Ready condition bravo, no combat void patrol unless the Cyrgal decide they want to get close. Guns uncharged but loaded. We need to be ready to fight, or run for the Crucible, at a moment's notice. And where the hell is the intelligence officer?"

****

Roland watched his torpedo's course on his HUD, the enclosure groaning and shaking as tiny grav thrusters adjusted the flight vector.

"Are we there yet?" Marc asked.

"I told you. When the torp shoots us out we'll be there. The only thing you have to do is to *not* ruin my focus," Roland said.

"This event you're describing seems indistinguishable from this suicide device being blown up," Marc said. "You might get lucky and just die. I can survive in vacuum. You think I want to become a hunk of space junk forever hurtling through the void until I slip into a gravity well a few million years from now? If I get lucky, it'll be a star and maybe—"

Roland tightened his hold around Marc's shoulders. The torpedo entered the atmosphere and shook with turbulence.

"Is that a good rattling?" Marc asked. "Or a that's-not-supposed-to-do-that rattling?"

"The Lady should have left you in your cell," Roland said.

"You know, you're not the first one to say that."

"*Templar,*" Martel said through the lance's internal channel, "*we're coming up on our release point.*" The HUD shifted to a pair of islands a dozen miles off a coastline, both a few dozen square miles and separated by a narrow channel of water. "*Nisei have the northern target. We're on the southern. Search and clear by pairs, call out grids as you move. Find the Aeon.*"

"Roger, sir," Roland said.

"*Ferrum corde,*" Nicodemus added, which the lance repeated after him. Roland's arm around Marc shifted as he tried to beat a fist against his breastplate in salute.

The HUD changed back to the torpedo's course just as it crossed over the ocean on final approach to the islands.

"*Contact,*" Morrigan said and a pair of threat icons appeared behind them, seemingly from out of nowhere.

"What are they?" Roland asked in channel.

"Sensors can't get a good reading through the torp's wake," Nicodemus said. *"Aircraft. Big. Almost the size of a Mule transport."*

The threats accelerated after the torpedoes, closing the gap slowly.

"There might be a problem," Roland said to Marc.

"How much of a problem? Am I about to burn up in orbit?"

"Mad dog!" Morrigan shouted and air-to-air missiles shot out of the pursuers and chased the Armor.

"Big problem," Roland said.

Data from the torpedo flashed across Roland's HUD as it released chaff and heat-flare countermeasures. The missiles continued, undeterred.

"Ready for emergency release," Martel said.

"We're not over the island," Nicodemus added.

"We're not going to make it. Stand by in three..."

"Can you float?" Roland asked Marc.

"Why would you even ask—"

The compartment opened to a blue sky with tall

thunderclouds in the distance. A pair of red dots wavered over the horizon…the incoming missiles.

"Wait! I'm not ready for this!" Ibarra shouted.

"Doesn't matter," Roland said as the torpedo convulsed, ejecting one of the Templar lance over the ocean. Ibarra squirmed as the moisture in the air froze his body against Roland's Armor.

Roland had a split-second warning before the torpedo spat him into the air. He locked his hand around Marc's upper arm and wondered just how strong the Qa'Resh material was. He shot out of the compartment and the jet stream hit him with a slap. He was vaguely aware of Marc screaming as he kicked his feet out and arced toward the roiling ocean below.

There was a flash and a thunderclap as the missiles annihilated the torpedo, sending flaming debris through the air toward the islands. Roland shot an azimuth toward the original landing zone and clutched his limbs and Marc to his chest right before he cannonballed into the ocean.

Water enveloped him and he shot his legs and arms out, yanking Marc like a rag doll. They descended almost a hundred yards before Roland's feet crunched against a coral reef and tiny blue fish swarmed him. He looked at his hand, and found Marc's arm still in his grasp and the rest of Marc attached to it. The silver man thrashed in the water.

Roland gave him a quick shake and Marc snapped his face to Roland. The silver man calmed down as his surface quivered and ice formed across his shell. Roland set him down on a patch of sand and a panel on Roland's forearm opened up. Marc took a wristband out and snapped it on.

"Can you hear me?" Marc asked, his words coming through the IR net faintly.

"Yes, stay close. It won't have much range under water." Roland looked up at the silhouette of shark-like bodies between him and the surface.

"This is why I did all my fighting from the boardroom," Marc said. "Through intermediaries that liked all this adventure and terror. I'm not a boots-on-the-ground kind of guy."

"You are now," Roland said. What looked like a rock the size of a small car scurried away from Roland's feet.

"'Pay no attention to the man behind the curtain' was my mantra." Marc took a tentative step forward and flakes of ice swirled around his joints. "This is not working. I'll freeze solid if I stay still."

Roland set his internal navigation system and got a magnetic bearing to the islands. He hoped there wasn't anything in the ocean floor that would throw off his readings, or they'd be underwater for a very long time.

"Come on." Roland grabbed Marc by the arm and swung him over his back. The man clung to the suit's neck servos.

"This is undignified," Marc said.

Roland walked forward, moving slowly as he sloshed through the water. Armor was anything but buoyant.

"You're keeping your composure so well," Marc said. "Maybe it's just because I can't see you. Are you freaking out a bit? Say yes. It'll make me feel better."

"No." Roland went around a coral structure that looked like the branches of a willow tree, the insides alive with hundreds of fish. "I did underwater operations on Nimbus, searching for the *Cairo*. A ship your—our—navy destroyed."

"It's not easy, is it? One day you're all Terran Armor hoah hoah break stuff, now you're Ibarran—" Marc squealed and squeezed Roland's servos tighter as an eel slithered past them.

"I am Templar. Always Templar. That calling never changed." Roland adjusted his bearing and made his way slowly through the water.

"Can we stay away from anything with teeth? You're a walking tank but I bet I look like a fishing lure to everything down here."

"What did you call me?"

"Armor! I called you Armor." He tapped his arm with the wristband against Roland's shoulder. "Damn thing. You know, I never anticipated the 'Templar' being a factor after the Ember War. Of course, all I wanted to do was win that damn thing and stop all of us from going extinct."

"You were there, on the Xaros world ship when the martyrs held back the darkness."

"I was. Came face-to-face with a Xaros Master too."

"Tell me about it," Roland said. "We've a ways to go."

"Since I'm totally dependent on you, I guess I'll oblige. There I was, no kidding…"

Chapter 6

High Overlord Bale looked out over the Kesaht shipyards built into a great belt around a moon of the conglomerate's main planet. His perch within the massive space station, *Indominus*, was part of his larger, private facilities on the station. Being in orbit was preferable to the irradiated deserts and domed cities scattered across the nearby planet serving as the spiritual heart of the Kesaht system. That rock wasn't much to look at, by Bale's reckoning. It was nothing compared to the lush jungles and soaring crystal peaks of the Toth home world.

A now dead and empty home world.

The shipyard ring around the moon was progressing far too slowly for Bale's liking, though the daily casualty reports from the crews assembling it told him the Kesaht were indeed motivated to finish. The Toth had built a megastructure around their home, ripping apart nearby moons and working for hundreds of years to build that triumph. The slaves and robotic workers in that edifice would have assured Toth domination of the galaxy once the Xaros were defeated.

But it was all taken away at the end. The memory of seeing the wave of light ripple around the planet once filled him with fear, a fear that sent him fleeing the planet and into uncharted space to get away from the threat. That the humans unleashed a beast of ancient nightmares on his people…he didn't think the humans had it in them. That the weapon, a Qa'Resh named Malal, had devoured every last living Toth on the world in a span of minutes had proven an amazing story to turn the Kesaht against the xenocidal humans.

Bale rubbed a nerve ending along the interior of his holding tank. The new filigree of Vishrakath gold decorating his exterior changed hues ever so slightly, even if the light was constant. Toth overlords had decorated their tanks to the point of ostentation. When one was but a nervous system suspended in a tank, it was hard to keep up appearances.

The Kesaht indulged him with works of exquisite (by their standards) art that tried to bridge the gap between Sanheel scrimshaw and Ixio paintings. While the two species held that they could blend their cultures together, it was always apparent which species an artist belonged to.

As for the Rakka…creating totems and fetishes out of the bodies of dead enemies rather appealed to Bale, particularly when that creation was from a human. Two such pieces hung on the wall behind his observatory; both were Rangers captured from a transport ship, and the Rakka had carved their crude language into their skin as a prayer to Bale. While he knew the smell bothered his attendants, Bale had no such problems inside his tank.

He felt only pleasure and hunger…and the inverse to those neurologic states of being.

One of the four claw-tipped legs that maneuvered his tank scratched at the deck. It had been almost a day since he'd last fed. His laboratory held a number of specimens taken from Kesaht raids. While his work was, on the surface, to integrate aliens into the Kesaht Hegemony through the universal-truth brain implants he'd perfected from legacy Kesaht technology, test subjects had a very high spoilage rate.

Feeding on humans was too dangerous. He saw what happened to Doctor Mentiq on Nibiru. Terran Strike Marines had put out bait, a seemingly normal one of their wretched species, but when Mentiq had fed on the Marine…Bale's nerves shivered at the memory of Mentiq's head exploding. A bomb. The humans had engineered one of their own into a bomb that would overload the mind of the Toth that fed off it. Any of the procedurally generated humans could be another such trap. So even though he himself could not enjoy dining on a human, watching the Rakka work over human captives was enjoyable in its own right.

The door to his observatory opened and his Toth warrior bodyguards emerged from their cloak fields, hissing a challenge at the Ixio that stepped into the room. The bodyguards were seven-feet-tall, muscular reptilians with four legs, all ending in dexterous feet suited for climbing the towering trees of the Toth home world.

"High Lord Bale," said the Ixio, going to his knees and kowtowing, "may this humble servant approach?"

One of the guards lifted a crystalline halberd over its head. Bale activated the guard's pain collar and its jaws snapped at air.

"Approach, Tomenakai," Bale said.

The Ixio kept his gaze to the floor and spread his thin arms to the side as he shuffled toward the glass wall.

"Please forgive me for intruding," the Ixio said. "Your instructions were not to be disturbed—"

"Unless you had news vital to the war against the humans," Bale said. "I know you're not an imbecile, Tomenakai, else I would not have Risen you to immortality to the Kesaht's service."

"A blessing that has persisted through my death," the Ixio said. "Our monitoring stations intercepted word of a Terran incursion into Cyrgal space."

"The Cyrgal…imbeciles. The only way to get more than one of their yammering kindred to work together is to light them on fire or blow a hole in their ship. Have the vile Terrans done something so spectacularly stupid as to attack a neutral world—particularly a world of *that* species?"

"The incursion has not turned violent to such a degree that the Cyrgal have declared a vendetta against the humans," Tomenakai said. "What is of more interest is which planet they trespassed upon. Ouranos. The protectorate of a species near extinction called the Aeon."

"The Aeon…" Bale's nerves twitched. Before he fled the destruction of the Toth home world, he'd been a trader in exotic foodstuffs for other overlords. The price for an Aeon was unlisted, a sale reserved only for Doctor Mentiq.

Bale activated the database within his tank and called up the old files. The Aeon didn't even have a flavor profile, which was highly unusual for Toth records. The only entry that meant anything to him read: Possess extensive Qa'Resh knowledge. Live delivery only!

The tendrils extending down from Bale's brain wrapped around his spinal column.

"A Qa'Resh expert? I didn't know such a thing existed," Bale said. "Why would—the Ibarras!"

"My lord?"

"The Ibarras have chased down Qa'Resh artifacts since they—and the rest of the humans—committed genocide and began their reign of terror," Bale said, remembering to keep to his script. "If they're risking a move into Cyrgal space, they must have found something truly remarkable."

"Shall we prepare an emissary fleet?" Tomenakai asked.

"One to carry the light of the Kesaht to the Cyrgal and destroy the Ibarrans out of course?"

"Not a Kesaht fleet," Bale said. "The Cyrgal are…difficult to manage unless prodded correctly. An emissary fleet might turn their entire species against the Kesaht—a risk we don't need while we continue the war against the murderers of Earth. No, we will send another fleet, one that has no direct attribution to the Kesaht."

"High Lord Bale," the Ixio said, "you can't risk—"

"Who said anything about me? I have-I have much to do here! Yes. Much too much to accomplish with the Kesaht…you, on the other hand…" Bale poked Tomenakai in the chest with a metal claw, nearly knocking him over.

"I arrived here many years ago with the last of the Toth," Bale said. "Spawning pools have replaced some of our numbers, but my warriors are a shadow of their former selves."

He sent commands from his suit on an encoded frequency he'd never shared with the Kesaht and a massive shadow cut over the moon. A Toth dreadnought, its hull resembling a coral reef dotted with energy cannons, came into view.

"You will take the *Last Light* to Ouranos," Bale said. "I want the Aeon alive, you understand? Alive. Raid Leader Charadon, my finest warrior, will assist you. And if you fail—"

"Never! Never, my lord." Tomenakai went to his knees to grovel.

"Charadon will rip your heart out and your Risen implants will send your mind back to me to explain your failure in person," Bale said.

"But that will mean the death of my body," the Ixio said. "The memory of the act is…"

The Toth warrior at the door hissed and snapped at Tomenakai.

"Then succeed," Bale said. "Go. What are you waiting for? Go! Bring me the Aeon!"

Chapter 7

President Garret tossed his suit jacket onto a leather couch in his office and slid his feet out of his shoes. He put one hand on a wooden desk, a faithful re-creation of the Resolute Desk from the long-gone White House Oval Office, and sat down in a beat-up chair that creaked under his weight.

His hands trembled, a palsy that lessened as he concentrated on holding them still. His body seemed to bleed energy into the desk and he felt like crawling to the couch to sleep. He hit a button on the inside of the desk and a small drawer popped open. A half-dozen pill bottles and foil blister packs rattled within.

His fingertips wavered over a green bottle, then he snatched up a small black vial in the back. Popping the lid, he shook out a glossy black pill with a red stripe around the middle.

"Hello, my pretty," he said, and the words came out as an exhausted rasp. His eyelids drooped and he shook out a second pill, then tossed them back and washed them down with a swig of whiskey from a flask on his desk.

That he enjoyed the occasional nip was no secret to his staff. The amphetamine use had kept up since the Ember War and been kept secret from all but his trusted Secret Service agents for years.

He leaned back in his chair, a holdover from his time as an admiral that had travelled with him from one ship command to another. He'd nearly lost it for good when the *Constantine* went down during the Battle for Ceres.

The pills took hold quickly, and he felt his energy surge. The shaking got worse, but now he could focus.

The door to his office burst open and a pair of agents rushed inside. Garret slammed his secret drawer shut and bolted to his feet.

"Mr. President, we need to get you to safety," an agent said. "Our out-system pickets detected a mass driver on course for Earth."

"How many and how close?" Garret slapped away the other

agent's hands when he tried to lead him away by the elbow.

"Protocol requires—"

"How many and how close?" Garret half shouted, composing himself before the question could become an outburst.

"One. Just past Neptune orbit," the agent said.

"I'll monitor from the war room." Garret went to pick up his coat, but his hand shook so badly he dropped it to the floor.

An agent slipped it over his shoulder while the other pressed a hypo spray to the side of the president's neck.

Garret felt like lead had flooded his bloodstream, but the palsy subsided. His men knew the drill by now.

He managed a quick but dignified pace to the war room. If the president were to be seen running or carried off by his protection detail, it would send ripples of panic through Camelback Mountain where the Terran Union's military was headquartered.

The war room had a large holo tank in the center and nearly two dozen officers manning workstations along the periphery.

A Ranger colonel saluted as Garret came up to the tank.

"Jackson, what have we got?" Garret asked.

"Single mass driver came out of an offset wormhole thirty-two AU from Earth." Jackson touched a panel and the trace came up in the holo tank. "Warhead masses five tons, but it's moving at—"

"How much damage if it gets through?" Garret asked.

"A thousand megatons equivalent," Jackson said. "Projected to hit Phoenix in fifty hours. The casualty projections are—"

Garret raised a hand and shook his head.

"Mr. President," said a Navy commander from behind him, "if it gets through, we'll lose the city. An evacuation ordered now will empty the city within two days."

"Listen to me. All of you." Garret leaned on the side of the holo tank to keep his hands from shaking. "We have spent the last two decades turning the solar system into the most heavily defended place in the galaxy. Bring up the macro cannons."

The holo changed to a top-down view of the solar system. The massive cannons, which used magnetic accelerators to propel warheads at near single percentages of the speed of light, appeared across the solar system—from the dark, scarred far side of the moon, Ceres, to hundreds on Mars and many times more across every geologically inactive body large enough to house the rings and the battery capacitors. Two space stations over Earth's poles came online, each with dozens of cannons.

"We have a firing solution?" Garret asked.

"Working up now," Jackson said. "We could make a low-confidence shot now."

"No. One shot, one kill." Garret swiped a finger down a control screen and the Keeper appeared in the tank.

"Sir?" Keeper's gaze wasn't on Garret as her hands flitted over control screens the president couldn't see.

"Where'd the mass driver come from, Keeper?" Garret asked. "And how'd it get so close before we detected it? You said the Crucible would disrupt any unauthorized wormholes out to Sedna."

"They slipped it in when I sent a troop transport through to Proxima," she said. "I'm honestly impressed they could do the math on the disruption wave. They detected when I paused the wave for the jump and opened the wormhole during the dip in quantum interference."

"How much of a problem is this?" Garret asked. "If we can't use the Crucible, the war gets real tough, real fast."

"Speed of light is our constant friend," Keeper said. "They can't slip a shot in like that unless I've got the Crucible open and they can't get any closer than Neptune."

"Fire solution loaded." Colonel Jackson leaned over and whispered the news. "Triangulation from three different macros ready on your word."

"Take it out," Garret said loudly and forcefully.

The holo tank switched to the entire system and three green dashed tracks appeared, all converging ahead of the incoming munition. A timer appeared next to the projected point of impact.

"Back to my first question," Garret said. "Where'd it come from?"

"The Crucible on the Novis colony," Keeper said. Her eyes didn't blink as screens reflected off her skin. "I'm getting…emergency transmissions from Novis. The Vishrakath have taken the system. The colony's been hit, badly."

"Alert the 17th Fleet. They'll retake the system," Garret said quietly.

A small grainy image appeared next to Keeper's screen: a picture taken from the inner ring of a Crucible, surrounded by hundreds of the converted asteroids the Vishrakath used as spaceships.

"That's a live feed. The 17th won't be enough," Keeper said.

"But…my crews in the Novis Crucible armed the Monkey Wrench before they were killed. We won't have much time before the Vish find the transmitter or the Wrenches. Permission to burn the bridge?"

"Granted."

"Fire mission sent to Mars." A half smile played across her lips. The red planet came up, along with the smaller Crucible orbiting the planet. A trio of macro cannons lit up on Mars, their mag launchers charging.

Every Crucible in human-controlled space was seeded with Monkey Wrenches—small, hard-to-detect denethrite charges designed to explode once a time-delayed fuse was activated. The explosions would render the gates too damaged to disrupt wormhole formation across their systems. At least until the Xaros devices self-repaired.

A wormhole formed inside the Mars Crucible, and another appeared just ahead of the Novis gate, slightly off-kilter. Three macro cannons on Mars shot hypervelocity rounds up from the planet and through the wormhole.

The camera feed from the Novis gate shook violently, and long, basalt-colored spikes went spinning through the void as the macro-cannon shells from Mars smashed it to pieces. The feed cut off.

"Gate kill." Keeper shook her head. "They'll repair it, but not for weeks."

"Their fleet's stuck there for now," Garret said. "This'll make them think twice before they move on another of our colonies."

"They're not stupid," she said. "They'll work out a countermeasure soon enough."

"How many people on Novis?" Garret asked, wiping sweat from his brow.

"Wait…" Keeper raised a chin to the screen and Garret looked to the converging tracks. He swallowed hard. A miss would mean a scramble across the solar system, and every macro cannon that had the time and distance to engage the incoming mass driver would come into the fight. With all the defenses Earth could muster, Garret could rationalize that he and Phoenix were safe. But the loss in confidence from a miss…

The timer ran to zero and a red triangle blinked over the convergence. Garret waited, not daring to breathe.

"It's a hit!" Jackson shouted and the room broke into cheers.

"Good work, Keeper," Garret said.

"We've only been rehearsing mass-driver interception every work shift across the system for fifteen years," she said. "They need to fire almost two hundred at once before I get concerned."

"All it takes is one to slip through," Garret said. He pulled the colony data for Novis up and the blood drained from his face. "I'll convene Congress in a few hours. Total war against the Vishrakath and their allies."

"I'll hold the fort up here," Keeper said.

The President of the Terran Union reached into his jacket and felt the pills hidden in a pocket. He'd stop by the restroom for a pick-me-up before addressing Congress.

Chapter 8

"Kid. Wake up."

Santos's limbs jerked inside his Armor's womb, feet and hands bumping against the inner shell as thick amniosis sloshed over him. He felt a slight tingle as the umbilical joining him with his Armor fed data into his brain.

Through the Armor's helm optics, he saw the Armor was still in the cemetery coffin. Chief Henrique and his technicians worked on the ground level, carting munitions around to the rear of the coffin where servo arms would load gauss shells into his internal magazines.

"Online," he said.

"Your sync rating's nominal," Aignar said through the lance's IR. Santos looked to the suit to his right. Aignar's Armor bore a fresh Iron Dragoon patch and bare swaths of graphenium on the torso and legs, a rush repair job that made the Armor look as if it bore battle scars.

"Cadre said it takes a few rounds of combat to fully meld with a suit," Santos said. "I should be in the green in no time."

"'Green,'" Aignar chuckled. "Mars shouldn't send bean heads like you straight to a fight like this. Cycling you through a lance that just came off the line is how it's been since the end of the Ember War."

"Reports from the outpost systems haven't been…positive."

"Umbra is an outpost world. You'll get to see how 'positive' things are pretty quick. We've got deployment orders. You checked out on the MEWS? Stupid acronym. First the tactical insertion torpedoes. Now 'Melee Enhancement Weapon System.' They should run the names by a twelve-year-old instead of some engineer weenie."

Santos pulled up a menu and a wire diagram of a hilt turned over and over in his vision. A blade extended and locked into place, then morphed into an axe head, then a gladius, then a pickax.

"Drilled extensively with them," the recruit said. "Lost our

Sundays off to close-quarters battle training. I never understood the reasoning. We're Armor. We carry double gauss cannons, rotary guns, the Mauser heavy rifle, and the rail system for killing starships in orbit. At what point did we decide to forgo all that ranged firepower so we could run over and hit an enemy on the head with a sword?"

"We must be deadly and capable at any distance," Aignar said. "The Corps neglected the up-close and personal fight for too long. The Ibarrans didn't. Now the Kesaht have their own Armor on the field and they have a 'close with and destroy the enemy' mantra that they don't deviate from."

"The Templar did focus on sword work. I thought that was just a nod to the Armor armed with Excalibur blades that fought the Xaros Masters at the end of the Ember War," Santos said.

"The Templar are gone from the Corps. Some of us learned hard lessons about melee combat. Captain Gideon will get you on the mats soon enough. Amazing what a few real bruises will do to aid muscle memory."

"You heard the rumor that the Ruhaald invented the tech to morph the MEWS from one weapon to another?"

"I heard. Ruhaald spent a lot of time working on anti-armor tech after the war. Word is the Iron Hearts scared the piss out of one of their brood mothers and the squids picked up a deep-seated fear of us. Can't imagine why. At least the Ruhaald are on our side in this fight," Aignar said.

"We've got the Dotari," Santos said. "And…the Karigole?"

"All two dozen of their warriors," Aignar said. "The Vishrakath bring a few more races into their alliance every month. Good thing every adult human in the galaxy served in the military one way or another. If the Union hadn't mobilized so quickly, the war'd be over."

"We're losing?"

"You're not winning if you're on the defense," Aignar said. "And here we are on Umbra. Our world. This ain't Cygnus, where we kicked the Vish off planet."

"The Ibarrans aren't much help," Santos said as he switched his view to a long, thick-barreled rifle mag-locked to his back beside the rail gun vanes recessed into his Armor. "It was nice of them to leave a few Mauser rifles for us to copy."

"The Ibarrans are another issue. Remember what I told you

about them and the captain."

"Not to speak of them unless I want my face ripped off. I got it."

"Do that, shoot straight, and follow your orders, and you'll be fine with Gideon…speaking of which, he's calling us to bay 37 for deployment. Ready to march?"

"Isn't that our lance motto? *Toujours pret?* Always ready?"

"You're not so bad for a bean head," Aignar said and the coffin pulled back from Santos's Armor.

He took a step and the techs began clapping. He looked down and saw a length of red rope with three knots around his right ankle.

"What's this?" he asked, reaching down.

"Don't!" Aignar shouted. "Bahia bands for good luck. Our techs are all Brazilians. The knots are some sort of old pagan tradition. Color means what kind of wish was done when they gave it to you. Don't take the band off yourself. When it gets burned or ripped off—and it will—the wishes will come true. Or that's what they say. I don't argue. They keep fixing my gear so I'm inclined not to piss them off."

"What does red mean?" Santos looked at Henrique and beat a fist to his breastplate.

"Strength and passion. Doesn't hurt to have that in a fight, though I could've used a four-leaf clover on more than one day. Let's move. Gideon's waiting."

****

Umbra passed beneath Santos's feet as the Dragonfly transport skimmed over the planet's surface. The undulations of the flight didn't bother him inside his Armor's shock-resistant pod, though if he'd been out of his Armor, he doubted he'd have kept his lunch down.

Santos ran landing calculations through his suit's systems. If the clamp around his waist suddenly released, he needed a plan before he was halfway down to a sudden stop against a mountainside.

"Santos, this is Gideon," came through his IR.

The young Armor looked over at his commander's suit in the harness next to his. The captain hadn't spoken to him or

Aignar since they loaded onto the Dragonfly inside the mountain base. Gideon had been in constant communication with higher echelons the entire flight, and Santos wasn't so green that he had to be told not to chime in to that conversation.

"Sir. Honored to be under your command and an Iron Dragoon. Let me—"

"I'm sending an operational overlay to you," Gideon said. "Tell me what you see."

A terrain map of Umbra came up in Santos's HUD. Blue rectangle unit symbols formed a roughly parallel line with red enemy diamonds through the mountains and valleys. A blinking cursor marked the Dragonfly, heading for where the lines met between a tall range. Santos zoomed in on the forward edge of the battle lines and worked his jaw from side to side in confusion. A symbol for a Ranger brigade was moving south, opposite a Kesaht division moving north.

"We're retreating," he said. "And so are the Kesaht…that's happening across the continent."

"Why?" Gideon asked.

"I don't…forgive me, sir. I don't know."

"The only true wisdom is knowing you know nothing," Aignar said. "But being clueless on the battlefield is a good way to be wise and dead."

"Umbra is a slow-rotation planet," Gideon said. "A full day lasts 211 hours. Long story short, the heat from the system primaries and the oceans on the other hemisphere make for some powerful Hadley cells. Hurricane-force winds and storms that'll last the better part of an Earth day are on the way. Maneuverability and survivability in that environment are a challenge. No air support. No evac. Neither the Kesaht nor our ground forces can operate, so the storm surge puts a temporary truce into play.

"There are bolt holes across the continent—caves and underground shelters for the original colonists—just big enough for a battalion of crunchies to fit into," Gideon continued. "Issue arises that neither we nor the Kesaht can field a large enough force to overwhelm the other. Put too many troops in the field, they'll get caught out in the storms."

"Stalemate," Aignar said. "We're bleeding each other dry without gaining any ground."

"Not a lot to eat in this place," Gideon said. "And like most wars, this will come down to logistics. Intelligence has 'high confidence' they've identified supply depots behind the Kesaht lines. If we take enough of those out, the enemy forward troops will wither on the vine."

"So this Dragonfly's going to drop us behind their lines?" Santos asked.

"In a big ball of flame and bloody chunks, maybe," Aignar said. "Kesaht air defense is too strong."

"High Command has most of our air assets on Yate's Star evacuating the civilians," Gideon said. "But removing eighteen million colonists isn't something that can be done quick and easy. We're not getting any more air assets for another three weeks at least."

"What's our mission, sir?" Santos asked as a waypoint appeared on the slope of a mountain in the No Man's Land between the Union and Kesaht lines.

"We stop these Kesaht from making it to safety, then fall back with friendly forces to the nearest shelter," Gideon said. "From there, we push out soon as the weather allows, see if we can't catch them in the open again. Force the Kesaht to spread themselves thin, find an opening to exploit to get into their logistics area."

"Sir, we are Armor," Santos said. "This plan strikes me as…cautious."

"It is," Gideon said, his frustration evident. "High Command wants the stalemate to continue. The longer we hold the Kesaht here, the more time we have to evacuate civilians. If the enemy lose their hold here, they'll push on another front. They're like bulldogs—soon as they bite, they don't want to let go."

"We're not fighting to win, Captain," Aignar said.

"There's a wider scope neither of you are thinking about," Gideon said. "Umbra is an outpost system. We're only here because of the system's Crucible. If the Kesaht get control of it, they'll use it to open a wormhole over Yates, New Denver, or Proxima, and shoot a mass driver through. Yates doesn't have the system defenses to survive that kind of attack. The other systems have a decent detection and destruction network, but it only takes one hit to ruin a planet."

A screen opened up on Santos's HUD. The edge was red and white chevrons with TOP SECRET in the middle of the video.

A ruined cityscape appeared. Ash fell like snow through a dark-gray sky.

"Novis," Gideon said. "Hit by a mass driver storm of almost twenty asteroids. Death toll is over nine hundred thousand."

"But Novis is to the galactic east," Santos said. "The Kesaht aren't attacking anywhere near there."

"It wasn't the Kesaht," Gideon said as the video winked out and a map of the galaxy came up, with a blue dot marking the Novis system. Ruby rings of nearby Crucibles appeared next. "Vishrakath and Naroosha ships seized the gates in nearby systems. They launched a coordinated mass driver strike before the colony knew what hit them."

"War's taken a turn for the worse," Aignar said. "The Kesaht want to kill us all, but they seem intent on doing it up close and personal, preserving the planet in the process. The Vishrakath just want to exterminate us all. If one asteroid the size of Manhattan hits a planet at the right velocity, you're looking at an extinction-level event across the whole place."

"We can't…" Santos felt blood rush to his face as anger blossomed in his heart. "When do we strike back?"

"The Union doesn't have enough ships to evac the outlying colonies *and* launch an offensive against the Vishrakath coalition," Gideon said. "Too many fires...not enough buckets."

"You'd think President Garret would abandon the Hale Treaty and reopen the procedural crèches. Get our manpower back up to the level where we—" Santos stopped as Gideon's helm snapped toward him.

"Did Knox and Mars spend a lot of time teaching you strategic-level thinking?" Aignar asked.

"No, sir," Santos said, silently thanking Aignar for the chance to step back from angering the commander. "Armor exists to win the tactical fight, to enable operational victories, thus allowing commanders flexibility on the grand scale."

"Concentrate on this fight," Gideon said. "We'll deal with the Vish in due time...stand by. General Kendall just opened a conference call." He left the lance network.

"Did I screw up?" Santos asked Aignar.

"We're in interesting times," Aignar said. "If someone thinks you're questioning the wisdom of part of the Hale Treaty, you're suspect against all of it."

"You mean the Omega Provision and the Ibarrans' illegal procedurals," Santos said.

"Christ…that," Aignar said. "That order's officially on hold. The admiralty almost went into open revolt after a summary execution on the *Ardennes*. Garret painted himself into a corner when he agreed to that part of the treaty. Of course, he didn't think we'd ever have illegal proccies in custody either. Damn the Ibarras. Damn all those that sided with those traitors."

The Dragonfly banked to one side and rose in the air, matching the slope of a mountainside passing beneath their feet. The release point icon on the HUD maps vanished.

"Change of plans?" Santos asked.

"Welcome to the battlefield," Aignar said as he cycled gauss shells into the double-barreled cannon mounted on his forearm, "where the enemy gets a vote and operation orders get tossed in the garbage soon as things kick off."

"But this means we'll be in the fight soon, doesn't it?" Santos asked.

"You learn quick, kid. I'll give you that," Aignar said.

Gideon joined the network again.

"Pathfinder observation post spotted a Kesaht armor column heading north through the valley. We're moving to intercept," the captain said.

Santos loaded his gauss cannons and an icy chill blossomed in his heart. He told himself it was just adrenaline, priming him for combat, not fear. Never fear.

A blinking diamond appeared ahead of the Dragonfly on the map, less than a minute away and just over a mountain ridge.

"Iron Dragoons," Gideon said. "I am Armor."

"I am fury," Aignar said, bashing a fist against his chest and causing the Dragonfly to wobble slightly.

"I will not fail," Santos said as he reached over his shoulder and gripped the handle on his Mauser heavy rifle.

The transport crested over a snow-covered ridge and the retro thruster flared, arresting its forward momentum. The clamps around the Armors' waists released and the lance dropped onto a pristine white slope.

Santos's feet sank into almost three feet of snow before crunching against rock. He loped forward, bounding down the mountainside, kicking up clouds of powder with each step.

Below, a wide, iced-over river snaked through the valley. Target icons sprouted up through the valley, the forward edge almost around a bend. Kesaht tanks were in the lead—massive, iron-clad war machines on treads with double-barreled turrets.

"Target lead elements," Gideon said. "Bottle them up in the valley. No mercy. No survivors."

Santos released the mag locks on his Mauser and flipped it over his shoulder and into his other hand. He marked a tank just behind the leading Kesaht vehicle and zoomed in. A Sanheel officer—a large, centaur-like creature with gold cords entwined in its long braids—was half out of a cupola, shouting at Rakka foot soldiers milling around the tank.

Santos lined up a shot, using his suit's targeting systems to compensate for the uneven bounds down the mountain. Sailing over a drop-off, he landed in a snowdrift that exploded in a cloud of white.

When he heard the crack of Aignar's and Gideon's Mausers, he cursed himself for not firing. His momentum carried him out of the snow and dislodged a shelf of iced-over snow, sending a segment of the slope the size of a baseball diamond's infield loose.

His vision cleared and he targeted another tank. He fired, the force of the Mauser's heavy shell blowing out a cloud of snow that melted and refroze into ice crystals an instant later. The Armor on the side of the tank flashed as the shell hit and the tank rolled to a sudden stop.

"Berserkers," Gideon said.

At the base of the mountain, a half-dozen deep-gray figures charged up the slope. The Kesaht had their own armor.

"Re-targeting," Santos said as a tank shell slammed into the mountain a few dozen yards behind him, pelting him with rock fragments.

"No!" Gideon said. "The lead tanks!"

"Rog—" Another shell exploded just ahead of Santos, slamming him to one side. He ducked into a roll, snow mashing into his every joint and his optics, but a quick blast of infrared and a jarring vibration from his helm's servos cleared his vision.

The valley was alive with Kesaht. Moving toward one side of the valley to face the Iron Dragoons were dozens of Rakka. The brutish foot soldiers carried long rifles and bore pelts over their shoulders along with fetishes of bones and souvenirs taken from fallen Rangers on their body armor. Sanheel officers towered over their Rakka soldiers, whipping them toward the fight and shouting in their crude language. Tanks slewed their cannons toward their flank.

The half-dozen alien armor continued their charge up the slope, bounding forward on all four limbs like a wolf closing on prey.

Santos took in the enemy force that seemed focused just on him and wondered if Captain Gideon had turned his first battle into a suicide mission.

"Get in close," Gideon said. "Grab them by the belt and fight."

"Novas?" Aignar asked as his Mauser boomed.

"Novas," Gideon said and a command prompt came up on Santos's HUD as he spun around a boulder. Tank shells bracketed his position.

He authorized the prompt and a shell popped out of the mortar tube integrated into the back of his Armor. Blast shields slapped down over his optics a split second before three Nova shells exploded, their light so strong it melted the top foot of snow around the base of the mountain.

The blast shields snapped up and the Kesaht floundered, pawing at their faces and flash-burnt skin. Tank turrets stopped tracking the Terran Armor, their vision slits blackened, their sensors overwhelmed by the Nova shells.

The Kesaht armor, who had their backs to the explosions, closed on the Dragoons, two for each of them.

Santos hopped forward and planted a foot on an ice-encrusted boulder. He fired his Mauser, hitting a tank in the thin rear armor and puncturing the ammo stores. It exploded into a shower of flame and twisted metal, scything through nearby Rakka and Sanheel.

A Kesaht armor lunged at him, its overlong hands ending in serrated talons that glinted in the twilight. The Kesaht's helm bore a mouth with jagged teeth that opened and screamed at him.

Santos leaned forward and jumped off the boulder. Tucking his knees into his chest and spinning over, he kicked his heels out and flew over the alien armor, his feet landing on the second attacker's shoulders. He knocked the Kesaht to the snowy ground with a crunch of metal and the Kesaht slid down the slope, Santos surfing on top of it.

Racking another round into his Mauser, Santos twisted his torso around on the Armor's waist gyros. He shot the Kesaht armor scrambling to catch up from behind, blowing a hole the size of a manhole cover in its torso.

The Kesaht beneath his feet grabbed him by the elbow and jerked him to one side. Santos fell into the snow, the Kesaht latched on to him, and the two iron giants pounded each other as they tumbled down the mountainside.

The world spun through Santos's optics, but he caught a glimpse of a tank square in his bumpy, chaotic path.

Santos braced the Kesaht armor in his arms and twisted hard, slamming the alien into the tank with a bell clang. His shoulder hit the Kesaht, and its body somewhat softened his impact. The alien armor let out a gurgle that sounded somewhere between pain and anger.

Santos rammed a fist into the Kesaht's face, crushing the helm against the side of the tank. The Kesaht's hand snapped open and four clawed fingertips slammed into Santos's torso, digging into the Armor's outer layer.

Santos punched his gauss cannon arm into the Kesaht's chest and suddenly remembered where the brain case controlling the suit was located. He fired a double shot and the shells blasted through the Kesaht, blowing a small crater in the ground. The Kesaht's claws popped out of his armor.

"Aignar? Gideon?" He looked over his shoulder in time to see a Sanheel drive a bayonet toward his helm. He ducked and swung his cannon arm up, deflecting the stab into the top of his helm. The point hit against the curved top of the Armor and Santos heard a fingernail-on-chalkboard screech as it scraped across.

Pushing off the ground with one leg, Santos drove his shoulder into the Sanheel. The Sanheel were big, massing nearly half a ton, but the impact bashed the Sanheel back onto its hind legs. The Sanheel glared at Santos, its fleshy face adorned with small gold rings, and spittle flew off its tusks.

It was the first time he'd ever come so close to another species, and all he saw in the alien's eyes was murder.

Santos activated the shield on his left forearm and swung his arm around in a hook as it unfurled. The reinforced metal edge sliced through the Sanheel's neck and popped its head up into the air.

"Captain?" Santos asked as he shoved the Sanheel's body aside.

A tank explosion flashed yellow light across the battlefield. Rakka milled about in near confusion, half-blind from the Nova shells. Smoke and flame bent off wrecked tanks as wind blew through the valley.

When a Rakka launched into the air from the other side of a rumbling tank and landed in a snap of bones next to him, Santos was fairly certain one of his lance mates was in that direction.

Bringing his rotary cannon onto his shoulder, Santos fired quick bursts into Rakka as he came around the front of the tank. The primitives were of little threat to him, and the more he cut down, the more the rest of them panicked.

He cleared the front of the burning wreck and stopped in front of an oncoming tank.

"Ah, balls," he said, diving to one side as one of the two turrets fired. He felt the rush of the shell scream by and landed on his flank. As the turret turned toward him, he fed a shell into his

Mauser and hit the tank in the treads, blowing through one side and out the other. The tank rumbled forward onto bare road wheels, leaving broken track behind it like shed snakeskin. The tank lurched forward, the leading edge of the armor digging into the ground, crushing one tube like a paper straw against a rock.

As Santos stood up and looked back to where Aignar and Gideon were still fighting, he heard the whine of hydraulics behind him. Spinning around, he saw the disabled tank's other tube aiming right at him. There was a blast and Santos went spinning as a shell the size of a football caught him in the side just above the waist.

The blow spun him like a top, slamming him against the ground and kicking up hunks of ice stained with Rakka blood. Static flooded his HUD and he felt the press of ice against his Armor through the neural link. His side ached—psychosomatic pain to match the damage to his suit.

When he tried to push himself up, it felt like red-hot razors tore down his spine. He was dangerously close to redlining. Overwhelming his body's neural systems with scrambled data from his suit would demolish his mind and send him into a coma from which only one Armor soldier had ever recovered.

His HUD cleared, and he looked up into a sky the color of an old bruise. His shoulder servos sprang back and forth, but his arms didn't move. Santos concentrated on lifting a hand, but the neural feedback turned into fire in his mind.

On an intellectual level, he knew he'd trained to recover from a battle-damage disconnect, but here, beneath an alien sky and in the midst of his first life-and-death battle, panic was on the verge of taking over.

Not now. Not here. I won't let Father be right about me! he thought.

A Sanheel bashed the butt of its rifle against his helm, making Santos's vision wobble. The alien loomed over him and drove a bayonet into the Armor's chest, the point sinking an inch into the metal before sticking. The Sanheel flashed a smile around its tusks and pulled it from side to side like a lever, digging deeper into the Armor.

"Time to die, demon!" the Sanheel shouted.

A pair of metal hands clamped around the alien's head, which exploded in a splatter of bone and maroon brain matter.

Gideon flung the Sanheel aside and stepped over Santos.

"Stay down," Gideon said as his gauss cannons barked and he loaded a shell into his Mauser.

"I can fight." Santos propped himself up, but Gideon stomped a heel against his chest and pinned him to the ground.

"Down! You're no good to anyone if you redline." Gideon's Mauser cracked and the recoil swayed him back slightly. "System reboot. Now."

"That takes—"

Gideon lifted his heel a bit and whacked it against Santos's chest hard enough to rattle him inside his inner pod.

Feeling his face flush with embarrassment, Santos relinquished his hold on his suit and reset his sync. If the Sanheel didn't overwhelm and kill Gideon in the next few minutes, he'd return to the battle with reasonable control over his Armor.

He listened to the fight around him. Shame nagged at him, and he wasn't sure if it was because he needed to be rescued or because he doubted his lance would save him when he needed them the most.

Neither answer was acceptable…and both could have been true.

Chapter 9

Makarov crossed her arms across her chest as she watched a single dot in the holo plot inch closer and closer to Ouranos. She activated the mag locks in her boots, heard them click and grip the deck plating, a nervous gesture, which wasn't a successful trait of flag officers and admirals. Every now and then, though, something slipped through the mask of command. Particularly when she was bored.

"Ma'am," Andere said, tapping at his workstation along the ring around the holo table, "we've got movement from the Cyrgal ship."

"How many hulls?" she asked.

"Just one, Admiral," the man said, swallowing hard, "but it

is something to see."

A green diamond flashed over Ouranos's inner moon. Makarov enlarged the spot with a flick of her fingers.

The Cyrgal ship orbited over a large city on the moon's surface, its hull the shape of a cone, the tip pointed toward the *Warsaw*. The surface was gunmetal gray and in uneven sections, as if the outer armor was made of wooden planks and bolted to the superstructure, while the cone tip was smooth and glowed with internal lights.

"Internal volume puts her at nearly eight times the *Warsaw*'s," Andere said. "We're on passive scans only, but there's no visible weapon systems."

"They slagged an entire Kroar raiding fleet," Makarov said. "They didn't talk them to death." She pulled up an overlay and electromagnetic emissions readings came up over the moon and Ouranos.

"The habitable planet is almost nothing but dead air," she said. "But the moon reads like there are millions of inhabitants. Why settle an airless rock when there's a paradise right there?"

"That's…" Andere frowned, "a tactical question I don't

have an answer to, ma'am."

"That behemoth hasn't moved on us since we arrived," she said. "They must consider protecting the moon more important than sallying forth for a fight. Which works in our favor. As soon as the extraction can get to the surface and back to us…we'll bid an Irish goodbye."

"A what, ma'am?"

"We'll leave. Just leave—before we mess something up and I have to send Guns down to the surface and he has to marry a chieftain's daughter. Maybe Gnarfle the Garthok. Something."

"Aye aye." Andere nodded quickly.

"Graviton detection!" came from the sensor station.

"From the Crucible?" Makarov lifted her helmet off her belt and slipped it over her head, locking it into place.

"Negative," the lieutenant said. "A Lagrange point near the third moon."

Makarov reoriented the holo tank…and stared at empty space.

"Brights?" Makarov asked, giving the sensor officer a sidelong glance and calling him by the nickname of his station, a tradition that went back to wet navy days.

"I'm certain of it, Admiral," the sensor officer said. "Readings are so large that there's no way it was a fluke. Shall I do an active scan of the area?"

"No." Makarov pressed her lips into a thin line. "Pinging the system is the first order in any long-range engagement. We can't do anything that could be construed as hostile. But a wormhole opening into the system with no ship…"

"Radar pulse from the Cyrgal," Andere said. "They saw it too."

A hail from the aliens pulsed in the holo tank.

"And here we go…" Makarov opened the channel with a flick of her fingers. Only six of the Kul Rui Gassla kindred came up in the tank.

"Explain," said the Cyrgal with the cyborg eye.

"We detected a wormhole formation," she said, "but it had nothing to do with us. What did you find?"

Squeaks and clicks that sounded like angry squirrels went between the Cyrgal as the *Warsaw*'s translation computers flashed with errors.

"We detect nothing," a hooded female said. "Wormholes do not open up by accident. This had to be an offset jump through a neighboring star's Crucible gate."

"I know as much as you do," Makarov said.

"The Aeon is ours to protect," a second female said. "The Tan Sar's claim will be overturned in adjudication."

"There is a single Aeon," Makarov said. "She cannot take up that much space. Why haven't you settled the planet? The risks and costs with a moon base are—"

"Ouranos is sacred ground," a scarred Cyrgal said. "The continents hold the dead. We will not defile it with our presence. Do not attempt another landfall."

"We're not here to start a colony," Makarov said. "Our business is with the Aeon."

Dozens more kindred joined the channel and a raucous cross talk began. Makarov muted her voice feed and froze the video.

"What do you think, Admiral?" Andere asked.

"Why would a wormhole just open? To send a mass driver through and wreck the planet with a hypervelocity ball of rock? A

Kesaht atmo scrambler? Such things aren't hard to spot…no…it couldn't be."

She opened a channel to the ship's engineering section and brought the bright screen lieutenant in on the call.

"Commander Montgomery," Makarov said, "can you generate a lepton pulse?"

The chief engineer, his face hidden behind the visor of his helmet, cocked his head to one side. "Short answer, no," Montgomery said. "Long answer, if I dissemble the fusion cores and we find a supply of uranium-232 to make a muon stripper then—"

"Heard," Makarov said, swiping the holo tank over to a single blue icon slowly approaching Ouranos.

"We can advance our timetable a few hours," Andere said. "But if we do that—"

"The Cyrgal will come gunning for us," Makarov said. "We need to walk on the edge of a knife to get the Armor and the Aeon off world safely."

"Shall we use the quantum dot to pass on the warning to Colonel Martel?" Andere asked.

"No…the Armor will be on high alert as it is. Marc Ibarra asked we hold back on anything that might jeopardize 'the pitch,' as he called it. The Lady agreed, and she knows that traitor better than anyone. This isn't an emergency…yet."

"What are we dealing with?" Eneko asked from the other side of the tank. "Shall we change our ready posture? Launch combat void patrol fighters?"

"Poker face, gentlemen. Got to keep our poker faces on," Makarov said. "Brights, how well do you know Karigole technology?"

Chapter 10

A current swept over Roland, carrying grains of sand across his feet and knees. He marched onward, noting the lack of sea life.

"You couldn't have gone back for them?" Roland asked.

"There was no going back." Marc bent an arm and a shard of ice broke off and was swept away. "We had one Mule to get Hale and company back to the *Breitenfeld*. Maybe one or two of the Armor could've made it out, but they were in the thick of it with the Xaros. You didn't see Elias and Carius, even in their Armor I could tell they wouldn't budge. They knew how that had to end. We barely got Torni out when we—"

Roland stepped on something metal. He lifted it up with the side of his foot—a blackened hunk of the insertion torpedo.

"You think the rest got out in time?" Marc asked.

"Yes." Roland let the debris flop back into the sand where it kicked up a cloud that was carried away and vanished into the ocean. "To die in such a way would be an embarrassment. The Templar lance's legacy will not trace from the last battle of the Ember War to an undersea accident."

"Can't all go like Elias. I saw him charge a Master, a giant black beast of an alien, and stab that monster in the third eye with—"

"Stop," Roland said. "My compass just went crazy. Must be the debris reacting to something in the water."

"So we…get out of the affected zone and figure out which way to go?"

"No use. The area will be enormous with the current spreading junk all over the place." Roland looked up at the surface. "I have an idea."

He plucked Marc off his back and grabbed him by the waist and shoulder.

"What are you doing?" Marc asked. "Wait. No. No. You are not going to—hey!"

Roland threw Marc Ibarra straight up like a spear. Marc shot through the surface and fell back through a few yards away. He sank like an anvil and hit the ocean floor in a cloud of dust.

Roland went over to him. "Which way?"

"I hate you." Marc struggled against the current to get to his feet. "Hate you so very much."

"Which way, or do I need to throw you again?"

Marc pointed into the depths. "Good news is we're close," he said. "Still hate you. Hope this seawater rusts your joints."

Roland swung Marc over his shoulder and continued on.

****

Light grew stronger as the water grew shallow as Roland marched through the ocean. He felt waves buttress against his Armor and saw surf breaking overhead.

"I think I can make it the rest of the way," Marc said and let go of Roland's neck servos.

"Stay here," Roland said. "I need to make sure the beach is clear."

"You know what Trinia looks like?" Marc asked. "There's

only one of her. It'd be a real shame if—"

"I know what Cyrgal look like. They're the threat...I don't know how the Aeon will react if she sees me."

"She knows all about Armor. Probably even saw that awful *Last Stand on Takeni* movie that had Armor in it...though I'm not sure how she'll take you standing on her beach." Marc widened his stance as the surf threatened to knock him off his feet.

"You think she'll be happy to see you?"

"Of course! We're old friends. Just haven't caught up in a while is all."

"Stay here." Roland walked in the direction of the waves. He ached to power up his gauss cannons or his rotary weapon, but the batteries of the gauss system wouldn't react well to water and firing through barrels filled with water would likely wreck his other weapon.

His helm crested the water and tiny blue fish wiggled out from the creases. Waves surged past him, obscuring his view of the beach. His optics were nearly useless as saltwater covered his sensors and flowed away again. He got a few glimpses of a white beach and a thick band of trees.

Roland cleared his head and shoulders out of the water and got a decent look around. To the left was nothing but a stretch of sand, no sign of civilization. To the right was a group of eight Cyrgal in blue robes clustered around a communication array bristling with antennae and dishes.

One of the Cyrgal held an oversized rifle across his waist with a pair of robotic arms that attached to a frame on his back. His true arms worked inside the array. The alien did a double take at Roland and shouted.

"Wait!" The word crackled out of his speakers as Roland advanced out of the water, waves splashing against the back of his knees.

The Cyrgal shouted as one, and all but one ran for a stack of rifles, stocks down in the sand.

Roland engaged his translation protocols. "I'm not here to fight," he said, his speakers whining, the Cyrgal language sputtering out.

The one Cyrgal with a rifle cocked his head to one side, then used his mechanical arms to heft up a rifle almost as tall as him.

"Blast it." Roland kicked the sand and sent a spray toward

the aliens, like an artillery shell had just landed on the beach. A plasma bolt shot through the sand wave and struck behind Roland. Searing bits of molten sand stung against his Armor.

Shaking seawater from his gauss cannons, Roland charged forward and came up on the Cyrgal, the plasma rifle's barrel glowing red-hot. Roland swiped a hand across his body and struck the weapon, intending to knock it out of the alien's grasp.

He did send it free of the Cyrgal's true hands, but the mechanical arms held firm. The alien went sailing through the air and slammed against an incoming wave. The other Cyrgal let off a keening noise and swung their plasma rifles off the pile toward Roland.

Roland drew his gauss cannons on the Cyrgal, but they didn't relent. He fired a single shell that pierced through two Cyrgal and struck the communication array. The device exploded into flames, sending shrapnel through the survivors and peppering Roland's Armor with fragments.

The aliens lay dead, blood seeping into the surf and streaming back into the ocean with the pull of the water.

"*Templar?*" came over the IR.

"Templar four," Roland said. He tried to triangulate the transmission and looked down the beach to the other island, where a thin band of water separated the two.

The IR crackled and his direction finders sent indicators from several directions as a thrum rose in the air. He turned around and saw the tall, bare-rock flank of a volcano at the center of the island. An aircraft raced around the volcano, wide wings swept forward slightly from the side.

Roland zoomed in. It was large, almost ungainly for something with so many weapons on it. A large turret on the top slewed toward him.

Roland engaged his targeting systems and fired a single round from his gauss cannons. The round struck at the base of the turret and sent the plane wobbling. It dove toward Roland, plasma bolts streaking out of the wings.

Roland ran to the side as the bolts slammed into the beach, sending up clouds of smoke and molten sand. He reloaded the gauss cannons and fired again, hitting just to one side of the cockpit.

The Cyrgal gunship rolled over and arced toward the other

island. The craft pulled back hard in a maneuver that a human pilot could never have managed without all their blood rushing into their feet, causing them to pass out. The smoking fighter flew back toward the volcano and crashed at the base, sliding up the flank and coming to a stop almost vertically against the rock.

"Maniac!" Marc Ibarra crawled onto the beach. "You could have called me. Throwing a Cyrgal at me isn't…good lord." He looked at the carnage in the sand.

"On your feet," Roland said as he sent an IR ping through the air.

A plasma bolt ripped through the tree line, igniting wide fronds as it passed, and struck the ocean in a cloud of steam.

Roland brought his rotary gun up, locking it against his shoulder, as he ran to Marc and sprayed the tree line. His bullets chopped through the foliage like a scythe.

"Templar four, head south!" came over the IR. *"Get across to the other island!"*

Roland scooped a cowering Marc into his arms and went running down the beach as plasma bolts stabbed out of the jungle. Roland reached his gauss cannon arm across his body and fired blind. Twin explosions followed by the groan of falling trees lessened the incoming fire.

His rotary gun swung around and sent a torrent of fire back and forth.

A plasma bolt sliced across his left leg and a jolt of psychosomatic pain went through Roland's body. He widened his stride and tore across the dozen yards of water flowing between the two islands. As soon as he crossed over to the other beach, the Cyrgal fire stopped.

Roland tossed Marc into a tall bush, flushing out a flock of multicolored birds, then he spun around and loaded a new magazine into his rotary gun.

"Cease fire! Cease fire!" yelled a Nisei, emerging from the jungle.

"There are a dozen hostiles—"

"They won't fire on us here," Umezu said. "They won't do anything that might endanger the Aeon. Deescalate."

Roland looked down at the line of melted Armor on his shin. Heat signatures in the jungle on the other island pulled back and he snapped the rotary gun off his shoulder.

"Marc?" he said, turning back to the bush.

"Help!" Silver limbs glinted in the sunlight as they waved in the air. Marc was on his back, broken eggs and bits of nest sticking to his body.

Roland pulled him out and set him on his feet. Marc looked down at his filthy personage, then back to Roland.

"You're welcome," Roland said.

"I take back every nice thing I ever said about you." Marc scraped bits of nest and frozen yolk off himself. "Which is nothing. But if I ever do accidentally say something nice, know that I—"

"Where's the rest of my lance?" Roland asked.

"No sign of them yet," the Nisei said. "You were the first one to exchange fire with the locals so they must not have reached that island yet. We're forty minutes from a thumper ping."

"Ran into magnetic interference in the drink," Roland said. "We should do the thumper now."

"Not standard operations." Umezu shook his helm. "They shouldn't drop anchor until two hours after the mission clock starts."

"Right...forgot," Roland said.

"Maybe they'll befriend a dolphin or something," Marc said. "Get it to do a peek-a-boo like I did."

"You find the Aeon?" Roland asked the Nisei.

"Not yet." Umezu sent an overlay to Roland's HUD. "Araki's holding his position farther inland. Our other pair is on the far coast."

"I'll take the VIP to the ruins in the center of the island, start a spiral out," Roland said.

"Thumper on the clock," Umezu said, then beat a fist to his chest and ran back into the jungle.

"Let's get off the beach," Roland said to Marc. "Don't want to be here if the Cyrgal decide this isn't neutral territory anymore."

Marc looked at the water and brushed his hands against his body. "Ugh, do you have a shower attachment somewhere in there?"

"Get moving."

Chapter 11

Roland pushed through a strand of fronds and onto a cobblestone road leading past domed-shaped buildings topped with points. The entrances were bereft of doors, the windows without glass or frames. The buildings were large—Roland could have stepped inside them if he ducked on the way through.

"Advanced civilization?" Roland asked Marc as he came out of the jungle, kicking mud from his feet.

"Once," Marc said, looking around. "So quiet. Can you use all that hardware of yours? Better than doing an Avon-calling impression."

Roland switched to his infrared sensors and found a heat plume at a small hut in a clearing just off the brick roads.

"There." Roland pointed to the spot.

"A thatch house?" Marc pulled his shoulders back and made his way over. Roland followed a few steps behind, gauss cannon arm cocked to one side and loaded.

They went past planted rows of bushes with stalks heavy with grain. Smoke drifted up through the top of the hut. A muddy slit trench ran around the hut and led out to the jungle pressing around the ruins.

Roland saw a shadow cut across a window. "Someone's in there," he said.

"Trinia!" Marc waved a hand in the air and stopped on the edge of a beaten dirt path leading to the hut's wooden door. "Trinia, it's Marc Ibarra…from Earth. Remember?"

"I thought you said she was your friend," Roland said.

"You be quiet," Marc hissed. "Those explosions were *not* our fault," he said louder.

The door creaked open. A woman—at least Roland thought it was a woman at first—stepped out. She was ten feet tall, hair like spun gold, and eyes a solid neon blue. Her skin was green, with a faint golden sheen to it. She wore a white tunic secured to her waist with a belt of twisted bark.

"I always said we'd meet some day." Marc tapped knuckles against his silver body. "Not bad, considering the circumstances."

"Leave," the Aeon said and slammed the door behind her.

Roland looked down at Marc.

"She's warming up to me," Marc said.

****

Scanning for targets, Roland sidestepped around a long building that had a single door parallel to bare stone the size of a hill. He continued along the hill, feet crunching against the cobblestones.

An incomplete triptych carved into the stone rose forty feet high, the first panel depicting Aeon gathered around a female that resembled Trinia. She stood atop a dais shaped like a topless pyramid, addressing those around her. A cloud in the background was oddly granular compared to the rest of the carving. He zoomed in and realized that individual Xaros drones made up the cloud. The Aeon were remarkably similar to humans, he noted, more so than any other alien species he was aware of.

The second panel was of the same public square, but empty of Aeon. The Xaros cloud had moved to the other side of the panel. The last third was bare rock—framed, but unfinished. He turned around, and there was the square and speaker's stand.

A pigeon drone launched out of the mortar tube on his back and sailed into the air with a *whoomph* as it left the housing.

"What are you doing?" Marc asked as he came over to inspect the massive carving.

"IR contact with the Nisei." Roland stepped off the cobblestones and sank his left heel into the soil. There was a whirl of a drill as the anchor in his leg bore into the ground. "No word from the rest of my lance yet. We'll coordinate anchor pulses through the ground. The other Templar should have dropped their anchors too. Depending on the terrain, we can transfer messages over a few hundred miles."

"Neat trick," Marc said. "Old Atlantic Union Armor used that during the war in Australia. Chinese never could figure out how your forbearers were coordinating operations without a beep of radio between them."

There was a thump as Roland's anchor spike beat against the

bedrock. Marc went toward Trinia's hut.

"Don't go out of sight," Roland said.

"Don't be a ninny. Ghosts can't hurt me and this isn't Indian country," Marc said as he turned a corner. "Don't need a nursemaid either," he muttered to himself.

He stopped at the edge of the dirt path to the hut, a wisp of smoke rising from the top. Marc touched the black box strapped to his wrist and a hologram projected out onto the path. Human children played in a park, the Phoenix skyline in the distance. Parents carried babies to picnic tables and a pregnant mother eased herself onto a bench.

The door to the hut opened and Trinia stormed out. She marched through the hologram and swiped at the projector, hitting Marc's elbow as he angled his arm to protect the device.

Trinia yelped in pain and clutched her hand.

"I need that!" Marc shouted up at her, the size disparity making it look like he was a child whining to an adult.

The Aeon shook cold from her fingers. "How did you get an ambassador body off Bastion?" she asked. "You were never even configured for those."

"I knew your curiosity would get you out of that hovel one way or another." He switched off the projector. "What are you even doing here, my dear? This wasn't the plan."

"The Xaros arriving on Bastion's doorstep and annihilating the station wasn't the plan either. I managed to escape just in time. Many more weren't so lucky—though *luck* is the wrong word for this." She turned toward the empty village.

"How did you manage?" Marc asked. "You came back through the probes to your real—much lovelier and disturbingly taller—body while the Xaros still occupied the system."

"Drones only sweep a planet every few centuries," she said. "So long as I lived primitively, they wouldn't have noticed me here. It was a bit of an adjustment after so long on Bastion…I forgot what a chore eating was.

"Then the Crucible gate in orbit opened and, after a year of living like this, the Cyrgal came through and told me the war was over."

"You can do better." Marc nudged a foot against a strand of the grain plants. It collapsed and snapped where his touch froze the stalk. "Sorry."

"I'm done, Ibarra. There's nothing left for me to do. The Aeon will extinguish with me, something that should have happened two thousand years ago, after the failure," she said.

"And if you'd given up back then?" Marc pointed up to the Xaros jump gate just over the horizon. "The gambit on Earth would have failed. We would have lost the Crucible those xenocidal drones built for us and we would have never made the assault on the Masters' world ship. The galaxy is free of the Xaros because of you. And me. I deserve some credit, don't I?"

"You took some convincing," she smirked.

"Realpolitik," he said, slapping his hands against his thighs. "That's a human word for accepting reality. I was a kid when we started working together on the procedural program, took me awhile to realize there was a narrow path to humanity's survival."

"Those images…are real?" she asked.

"They are. Human children are all over the place. Babies from procedurals are indistinguishable from any other babies. You did it. You saved us…you really can come and see them like we talked about. Not on *Earth*, just yet. I'm persona non grata there…for now."

"How is Stacey?"

Marc mumbled and took a few steps away. "She didn't take well to learning this—" he knocked on the side of his head, "—was what she was in while on Bastion. Everyone involved with her—you included—knew it would take time for her to accept her consciousness, and not her body, being sent back and forth to Bastion. She found out the truth during the escape from the Xaros attack and didn't take it well. Then her body was badly injured and my probe and I had to transfer her back into her shell to keep her alive. She's…struggled."

"And your body? You were resident in your probe last we spoke."

"Pa'lon's," Marc shrugged. "The old Dotari ambassador. He and Stacey came back to Earth in their ambassador bodies. Special Qa'resh design meant to solve diplomatic rapport problems. My probe put him back in his beaky body and I had to coopt this one to save Stacey. Real mess of a day."

"You're doing better for yourself than I would have guessed."

"Thanks, I think."

"Tell me why you're here."

"That's…a bit complicated. The procedurals are flawless, but the rest of the galaxy's threatened by them. I'm here for two reasons. First, we need your expertise with Qa'Resh tech."

"Leave. I know all about the war between Earth and the Vishrakath coalition. The Qa'Resh didn't leave anything behind that can help you with that, and I'd rather not be known as some mad scientist half the galaxy will vilify no matter who wins that fight. The Aeon will be known for our part in the Ember War, as you call it, and that will be the last of us."

"You worked for thousands of years to win that fight and now you're just going to give up?"

"We won, didn't we? Why can't I take my rest?" She knelt and plucked a weed from the rows of grain.

"Because of what I promised you…and because we found a Qa'Resh Ark," Marc said.

"Impossible." She threw the bit of weed at him. "They left nothing but garbage behind after their ascension. The lone Qa'Resh that stayed half in and half out of their dimension said as much."

"They left one of their own behind, that monster Malal." Marc paused. If he had a spine, a shiver would have run up it at that name. "Turns out he had a few things hidden from the Qa'Resh, and one was an Ark—one of their ships, with jump engines and all their technology, buried in a dark sector of space. And we know where it is."

"Then you have it?"

"I didn't say that. Even if we had the Ark, it's possible Stacey wouldn't be able to operate it fully. You know how difficult their language is. You worked with it for millennia. No one knows their technology better than you. Which is why we need your help."

"And what would you do with the Ark? Burn any world that threatens you? There's enough war as it is. I'm not going to help you."

"What did I promise you?" Marc moved closer to her, stopping short of the plants for fear of freezing and killing them.

"It's impossible."

"It was possible on Bastion but the station wouldn't let you even try. If we get the Ark, then—"

"No! The Aeon are gone." She stood up, towering over

Marc, her fists shaking with anger. "I killed them all and that is the end of it!"

She spun on her heels and headed back to her hut.

"We can bring them back!" Marc called after her. She slammed the door and he started down the path with a huff.

Pushing the door open, he found her curled up on a straw mattress. She grabbed a metal pan and threw it at him. It bounced off his head with no effect and clattered against the ground.

"I know what it's like," Marc said, "to be the one person who can guide everyone you've ever known, or could ever know, through that eye of the needle. Through an extinction event. I am the only person in this galaxy that's managed it, but you could be the second. I'm offering you hope and a promise, Trinia. Help us get the Ark and we can bring your people back."

"No…" She shook her head. "There's no guarantee it's even possible."

"*You* created the technology for the mind transfers through the probes to Bastion. *You* saved the Alliance after the Toth almost destroyed it all those years ago. *You* broke the code on the human genome to grow adult bodies in a mere nine days. *You* developed the procedural-consciousness computers. *You* did all that on the back of research that you did for your own people. You think Malal's Ark won't have the tech to do what I promised with you at the helm?"

"I'm a farmer now," she said. "I grow grain and fruit well enough. This is all I want now. I succeeded with your people. I failed with my own. It's time to let the past go."

Marc sat on the foot of her bed and it creaked like the wood was about to shatter. He looked around the room: simple clay oven, a pile of beaten metal plates and bowls, a half-sewn tunic that looked inundated with mold.

"This is depressing," Marc said. "This past bit, my own digs weren't exactly five-star, but you deserve better than this."

"I was a biologist and computer scientist on Bastion for several thousand years," she said. "Not a carpenter or a baker."

The hut shook as Roland approached. "Ibarra?"

"Here!" Marc held up a hand. "I'm fine. Don't break anything."

Roland bent over and looked into the hut, his helm nearly filling the window. Trinia scooted back against the wall.

"He's a puppy." Marc waved a hand at her. "A big metal puppy bristling with weapons, but he's my puppy."

"I made contact with my lance," Roland said. "They'll arrive in less than an hour. Is she ready to go?"

"*She* isn't going anywhere." Trinia threw a tin cup that bounced off the Armor's chin. "I thought you humans would be a little more…corporeal than this."

"The Cyrgal are active on the other island," Roland said. "The Nisei are moving to intercept them."

"Oh no, you don't." Trinia got up and brushed herself off. "The Tan Sar are cultists. I'm coming with you to stop any more bloodshed."

"Dangerous," Roland said.

"I am in absolutely zero danger with them," she said. "If you decide to start shooting, I'll be in even more danger than your mere presence is causing me. It's a miracle the Tan Sar haven't moved in yet."

"There's more than one kind of Cyrgal?" Roland asked.

"You couldn't have birthed humans with a bit better understanding of their enemies?" she asked Marc.

"He's not one of mine," Marc said. "His strengths aren't in diplomacy."

"A true-born human's in there?" Trinia left her house and went to Roland. Her head came up to the middle of his chest. She looked him over then reached for the Templar cross on his shoulder.

Roland pushed her hand away before she could touch it.

"More...crude than I envisioned," she said. "Come. To the channel."

"What's she talking about?" Roland asked Marc as they followed her down the path to the beach.

"You think Marc Ibarra designed your suits?" Trinia asked over her shoulder.

"It was my idea!" Marc brandished a finger at her

"I thought Dr. Eeks designed our plugs and the interface," Roland said.

"She holds the patent but Trinia did some of the work," Marc said.

"*Some?*" The Aeon walked faster.

"You know who's the only kind of person with an ego

bigger than artists?" Marc asked Roland. "Inventors."

"Did she design the graphene batteries you got famous for too?" Roland asked.

"Nope, that was all me. Well, the final design was improved upon ever so slightly by someone else, but I would've figured that all out on my own in no time," Marc nodded.

"Scientists," Roland muttered.

Chapter 12

Makarov reached into the holo tank and touched a blinking icon on a vector to Ouranos's atmosphere. A timer appeared, counting down several more hours.

"XO, give me combat status on the fleet," she said.

"The frigate squadron is at ready station one," Andere said. "Rail batteries loaded but uncharged per your instructions. They can have rounds in the void in ninety seconds from receipt of a fire mission. Destroyers are in a perimeter screen, but the Cyrgal haven't sent anything our way…yet."

"The wait's getting to the crews," Eneko said. "Are the Cyrgal going to fish or cut bait?"

"Quick decisions and violence of action don't seem to be traits of their species," Makarov said. "Everything is done through committees. Progress must be glacial…if at all."

"Intel says it takes a clear and present danger to get them out of gear," Andere said.

"That may be what we're dealing with." Makarov zoomed out from the icon to the local space around Ouranos. A dashed red line traced from the planet to the place where the rogue wormhole appeared. Several different red diamonds for possible enemy locations dotted the projected course.

"XO, execute maneuver plan Theta if there's a radical change during this call. Comms, open a channel to the *Concord of Might*." Makarov removed her void helmet and mag-locked it to her thigh.

The entirety of the Kul Rui Gassla kindred appeared in the holo tank.

"Your status is in discussion," said the male with the cybernetic eye. "Several kindreds are engaged in marriage talks to form a stronger voting bloc. We should have a resolution in the next nine days, unless the Fan Tara appeal to the home world for adjudication. In which case—"

"A lepton pulse," Makarov said. "Can you generate one

from your colony or your ship?"

The image of a female with a veil across her nose and mouth came to the fore of the holo tank.

"We can," she said. "A strange request. One that would require the kindred to renegotiate from the beginning to incorporate this new information...if it's granted."

"I am never ordering a pizza with the Cyrgal," Andere muttered.

"The wormhole remains an enigma," Makarov said, "one that has me concerned for your colony's safety."

"You're aware of a threat?" another male asked. Three more kindred appeared in the tank, all silent and focused on the Ibarran admiral.

"Not from me or my fleet," Makarov said. "We are here to talk, not to fight."

"The Tan Sar suffered casualties from your iron giants," the cyborg said, "but they are fanatics, cleaved from the whole. Let them suffer."

"My Armor acted only in self-defense, I'm sure." Makarov felt her cheeks flush. The few messages they'd received from

Martel on the surface were terse, relaying only that they'd made contact with the Aeon and hadn't suffered casualties. The extent of the damage they'd caused on the way in hadn't made its way into the report. She made a mental note to have a discussion with the former Terran Union Armor commander regarding Ibarra protocol once he returned to the *Warsaw*.

"Why a lepton pulse?" the veiled Cyrgal asked. "There is no known interaction between leptons and wormhole phenomena. The Aeon civilization thrived for many millennia. All potentially hazardous comets and asteroids were culled soon after they gained space flight."

"It has to do with what came *out* of the wormhole," Makarov said, "not the wormhole itself."

"You're aware of a threat?" the cyborg asked.

"I...suspect a threat." Makarov brought the projected course from the rogue wormhole up in front of her face for the Cyrgal to see. "Depending on the initial velocity, a—"

The Cyrgal in the holo burst into animated discussion. Makarov pressed her lips together in frustration and held up both her hands.

"On Earth," she said loudly, "we encountered—"

The kindred vanished from the holo and Makarov dropped her hands to the railing surrounding the tank.

"How did Lady Ibarra deal with this all those years she was an ambassador?" she asked, not expecting an answer.

"Any change to our posture?" Andere asked.

"No." Makarov shook her head. "Comms, get a quantum dot message to the Armor. Tell them to hurry the hell up before this system blows up in our face. We have a few more hours before the situation comes to bear."

Chapter 13

Santos raised an arm up over his face and looked at his Armor's hand as he tapped digits against his thumb tip. The sky had darkened further, almost on the cusp of night.

Rolling over, he saw his Mauser beneath the headless Sanheel's body. He yanked it free and stood up.

The battle was over. Smoke wafted out of burnt-out tanks and alien bodies were strewn about. A strong wind blew sheets of snow down from the mountains, whipping it into a light fog of ice particles.

"Don't move," Aignar said as he came up behind Santos. Aignar brought a fist up to the base of the other Armor's helm and a data line snaked out of Aignar's wrist and into a port just beneath the inches-thick plating on the helm.

"I'm sorry," Santos said. "I shouldn't have—"

"Stow it, kid," Aignar said. "You're alive…and in enough pieces you can still fight." He tapped the side of Santos's Armor and the jagged hole that was there, the edge rimmed with cracked graphenium and still warm.

"A couple inches to the left and I'd be thanking your corpse for the ammo," Aignar said. "I've come away from a fight in worse shape. Your system checks out. You get a double optical feed or feel tingling in your extremities, full stop. Understand?"

"I got it," Santos said. "Where's the captain?"

Thunder echoed off the mountains, the round of bursts from a rotary cannon cutting through the wind.

"He's finishing off what's left," Aignar said. "Most of the Rakka broke and ran for the hills. They won't make it through the night."

Gideon emerged through the haze, smoke wafting out of his weapon barrels.

"He check out?" Gideon asked.

"I'm good to go, sir," Santos said, hefting his Mauser up into both hands.

"I didn't ask you," Gideon growled.

"Eighty percent solution." Aignar withdrew the data cable from Santos's helm. "Give him a couple minutes for his suit to work around the damage."

Gideon pointed to a spur on the other side of the valley.

"There's a cave over there," he said. "Storm came in faster than anticipated. No evac until full night. We shelter in there."

"We're not going back?" Santos asked.

"It's egg loaf night at the mess hall," Aignar said. "You're not missing anything."

"Move out." Gideon ran toward the spur and his lance followed.

Santos winced at his uneven gait. The soldier within a suit was keyed to an undamaged system. When the Armor had to compensate for a lost limb or wrecked servos, it had to adjust the link into and out of the soldier. Santos was able to run normally, though he still felt a stich in his side from the Kesaht tank shell.

The cave opening was only wide enough for one suit to enter at a time.

"Before you ask," Aignar said as he watched Gideon go

inside, "it's not the wind and a little rain that's a problem." He flicked the rail gun vanes behind his shoulder. "It's the lightning. Getting hit with that is about as fun as a kick to the huevos."

"Clear," Gideon said.

The cave was a little larger than a Mule cargo bay. Small mounds of blown snow clung to rocks within. Santos aimed his gauss cannons at a dark passage beyond their chamber.

"Think any Rakka made it in there?" he asked.

"How can you answer your own question?" Gideon asked.

Santos switched on his IR filters…and saw no residual heat of a Rakka's recent passing.

"Roger, sir," Santos said. "Got it."

Aignar entered the cave and moved to the back as Gideon posted himself as sentry at the entrance.

"Field repairs," Gideon said. "Santos, link me your camera footage. We've got at least nine hours until the storm passes."

Santos opened menus on his HUD and sent files to the captain. He was tempted to ask what he was looking for, hoping for a chance to explain his less-than-stellar performance on the battlefield, but he opted for silence.

"Your mortar's out of alignment," Aignar said to Santos. "Hold still." An arc welder and drill bits popped out of Aignar's forearm housing and as he went to work on Santos's back, Gideon dropped off the network.

"I'm done, aren't I?" the junior soldier asked.

"Why would you be 'done'?" Aignar asked.

"I...failed. Almost got killed. The captain had to pull my ass out of the fire. I was a liability in a fight...I'm such a waste."

"I don't remember the captain saying, 'And if you come back with one ding on your Armor, you'll be back on Mars peeling potatoes with Cookee.' You hear him say that?"

"Doesn't matter. I screwed up."

"You got tagged." Sparks flew off Santos's back as Aignar kept working. "I saw you alley-oop over that Kesaht armor and take them both out. Bet you'll remember where they keep their brains next time. We didn't kill every single tank, but we got most of them. The Rangers down the valley will appreciate it."

"How many got away?"

"Not exactly sure. That's why the captain wanted your footage."

"Oh."

Aignar stopped his repairs for a second, then the sparks flew again.

"What is it with you, kid?" he asked. "I checked out your training records soon as we heard you were inbound. Traded notes with your senior instructor, Lieutenant Chapman. He wasn't surprised you were assigned to us. Good marks all around. I thought he was joking when he mentioned a complex."

"Complex? What complex?"

"You think your cadre don't know you?" Aignar glanced over at Gideon, silent and immobile as a statue at the entrance. "Course, Gideon and Tongea were our cadre. Not really helping my point, am I?"

"I don't know what you're talking about," Santos said.

"You know what? I'm not the one with a hole in my upper casing, so you get to go into receive mode for this conversation." Aignar whacked the ball of his fist against Santos's Armor. "Wish Cha'ril was here. Her Dotari sensibilities tend to cut through regular, old human problems. Unless it's her Dotari-ness that's causing the problem. Stop distracting me."

"Sir, I am so confused right now." Santos considered opening the channel to Gideon for help.

"I like to talk when I work. Your mag accelerators are misaligned. If I don't fix them, the next mortar you shoot will go helter-skelter. You'd think 'close enough' would be OK for mortars…until they land on your head."

"Reads fine to my HUD," the young Armor said.

Aignar slapped the side of his helmet and amber-colored alerts appeared on Santos's HUD.

"I spoke to your cadre," Aignar continued. "They said you're more than capable…but you don't feel like you deserve your plugs or your suit. Yet you were never at risk of being a lack-of-motivation drop."

"They said that? I don't…I don't think that's relevant, is it? You think I'm going to dump my fluid right here, right now and just walk off the battlefield? I've been shot and stabbed. My motivation's pretty high right now," Santos said.

"You were spiraling into self-pity a few minutes ago. I can't afford to take anyone for granted anymore and I don't care if you find my lack of faith disturbing. Why Armor? Why not drop for something cushy like logistics or babysitting a macro cannon out in the Kuiper belt?"

In his pod, Santos's shoulders slumped. He realized his arms had been clutched to his side and his knees locked together. He pulled his consciousness away from his suit for a moment and focused on the sensation of the amniosis enveloping him.

"Kid?"

"Sorry. It's…sort of a secret. I'll tell you, but you need to keep it quiet, OK?" Santos asked.

"It is *not* advisable to keep anything from Gideon right now. Or the Corps. Or the Union."

"It's not some sort of security concern. At all. It's just a bit…my father. I went Armor because of my father," Santos said. "I asked him which branch I should join and he said any but Armor."

"Hell of a reason to get your plugs."

"Of all the branches, you'd think he'd respect Armor the most. He was *there*, on the Xaros world ship, when Carius, the Iron Hearts, and the Hussars sacrificed themselves," Santos said. "But this is the only place he didn't want me."

"Wait, your dad was on the *Breitenfeld*?" Aignar asked.

"No. He was airlifted off the world ship before the annihilation bomb went off."

"Can't be. Your name's not Hale or Standish or…who else was there?"

"Orozco."

Aignar's welders and tiny servo arms pulled back from Santos's mortar tube.

"Orozco? The spokesman for Standish Liquors? But your name's not—"

"My parents weren't married. He wasn't exactly around when I was growing up. Then again, he had a lot of other kids to keep track of," Santos said.

"I thought all those paternity suits were some sort of gag," Aignar said. "Part of his brand."

"They're real. Mom and I weren't hurting for money, but every time he got a twinkle in his eye, I swear the pie got sliced a little thinner. He wasn't around much. He'd stop by for birthdays and crap like that, but he was never a father in any real sense," Santos said.

"I bet seeing Dad on vid ads and billboards holding booze bottles must have been frustrating," Aignar said, going back to work.

"You get it. Orozco was there when the Armor won the Ember War. He saw them dying just before the bomb went off. He didn't want that to happen to me. But to hell with what he wanted. He wanted to be my dad? Should've cared about me my entire life, not when it came time to bother him."

"I'm divorced from my son's mother," Aignar said. "Marrying her was a mistake, but being his father isn't. Orozco never married anyone?"

"Never."

"How many half-brothers and sisters you got?"

"Something like thirty-six."

"Holy—does that include you?"

"Thirty-seven bastards," Santos said. "And it did make dating a bit complicated, always wondering if that cutie with Spanish eyes and blond curls might be another souvenir of Daddy Orozco's conquests."

"Damn." Aignar closed up his tools and a blow torch

snapped out from beneath his wrist. "I didn't know you were a little famous. Drop me a pair of graphenium ingots from your maintenance kit. Time to get rid of that Kesaht marksmanship tag on your torso."

****

Water ran off the cave opening in thick streams, almost forming a waterfall as Santos stood guard at the entrance. There hadn't been much to see in the last few hours other than the deluge. A stream rushed past his feet and deep into the cave complex. That their space hadn't flooded yet hinted at a vast network of voids beneath the mountain.

He rolled his shoulder servos backwards and forwards, testing their resistance to the command impulses through his spike and neural interface. His Armor read as fully mission-capable, but he felt a slight lag every time he moved.

"Mr. Santos," Gideon said, addressing him with his warrant officer rank.

"Sir," Santos said, keeping his optics on the entrance and the storm beyond.

"Tell me what you see." Gideon sent a holo vid to Santos's HUD. Footage from his weapon camera was spliced together with feeds from Aignar and Gideon. Santos grimaced at how shaky his video was compared to the other men's. The opening moments of the ambush in the valley played out in a loop.

"Our assault on the Kesaht," Santos said.

"Good thing you didn't go out for the Pathfinders," Aignar said. "Powers of observation like that…"

"Look closer, Santos," Gideon said. "Look at the forwardmost tank."

Santos froze the playback and enhanced the few frames of a tank at the head of the column—a tank that Santos had marked off as his target before Kesaht shells and their Armor fouled his shot.

"The markings are more ornate," Santos said. "Two different alphabets on the cupola. Rakka cuneiform and the circle script of the higher castes…none of the other tanks have that."

"And the Sanheel in the cupola?" Gideon asked.

Santos pulled out screen captures of the alien, whose head and shoulders were visible for only a few seconds before it ducked inside the safety of the metal vehicle.

"Looks just as ugly as the rest of them," he said. "The gold bands worked into the ponytail are different." He pulled out two frames of separate angles of the back of the Sanheel's head. A wide silver clasp ran along the base of the skull, and the flesh around the edge was scarred and puffy.

"Kesaht all have some level of cybernetic augmentation to their brains, yes?" he asked. "Modification to the language and perception tissue. Don't Sanheel have their augmentation over their left ears?"

"Told you he'd spot it," Aignar said.

"He sees the forest, not the trees," Gideon said. "That is a Risen, Santos. One of the Kesaht's senior commanders. Risen are priority targets. Our mission just changed."

"That tank escaped." Santos felt a bit of ice lodge in his chest. "If I'd made my shot, then—"

"Fate smiled upon us," Gideon said. "If you'd killed the Risen, it wouldn't have done much for the fight on this planet. That it got away may help us win the entire war."

"Sorry, sir, I'm a bit confused. *Not* eliminating the Kesaht commander was a good move?" Santos said. "I distinctly remember my training on Knox and Mars boiling down to killing aliens and breaking their things."

"Risen are immortal, to a degree," Aignar said. "We first encountered a Risen Ixio on Oricon. When Ro—our lance—killed it, the cybernetics in its skull sent off a wide-spectrum data stream that traveled through the system's Crucible."

"Military intelligence is certain the data was a backup of the Risen's mind," Gideon said, "and the data went to the Kesaht's home system…a location we don't have yet. We need to get word back to the Keeper, the specialist that controls the Crucible over Earth. If she knows a Risen transmission is on the way, she can track the data back to its final destination."

"We'd have their home world," Aignar said. "We'd have a place to strike. This whole war's been us trying to put out fires on one system after another. We can finally go on the offensive."

"First the Kesaht," Gideon said, "then we'll find Navarre and end the Ibarrans."

"So I may have inadvertently helped win the war?" Santos asked.

"Don't make a habit of screwing up and expecting a pat on the head," Aignar said. "Just don't."

"We need to get word through this system's Crucible, then find and kill the Risen," Gideon said. "We caught that one in the open. Rattled him. He'll be more cautious now."

"Surrounded by more tanks and more of their bastardized armor," Aignar said.

"Then how do we find him?" Santos asked.

"We make him come to us," Gideon said, pointing to the cave entrance. "Most of the lightning dissipated after the storm front passed. We move out now. I have a plan that should work."

"Sir," Aignar said, flicking a rail gun vane, "I would like to respectfully note you said *most* of the lightning."

"I didn't say the plan was a hundred percent safe." Gideon shrugged. "But if the enemy believes we're too cautious to move in this weather, then we're more likely to catch them off guard. We are Armor, not infiltrators or partisans. But this is the hand we're dealt."

"Enough violence can solve any problem," Santos said.

"See, sir," Aignar said, "I told you the kid had his heart in the right place."

Lightning crashed and thunder rumbled through the valley.

"Follow me." Gideon pushed past Santos and into the storm.

Chapter 14

"Admiral!" Andere tapped at his control screen and the holo tank snapped to the enormous Cyrgal ship, the *Concord of Might*. Sections of the outer hull had broken off and were slowly floating away from the ship, like pieces of a puzzle coming undone.

"Are they hit?" Makarov asked. She raised a finger to Eneko, who had his hand to an ear and was ready to execute a fire mission across the fleet with the press of a button.

"No atmosphere loss," Andere said. "And…that's odd. The sections are still connected to the ship."

The holo zoomed in on the alien ship. The hull fragments were almost the size of an Ibarra destroyer, some as large as a cruiser, and all were tethered to the main ship through enormous umbilical lines as thick as a hab building on Navarre.

"The cables are heating up," Andere said. "I don't have an—"

"Plasma conduits," Makarov said. "The hull sections are their weapon systems."

"Tube ports opening across the ship's hull," Eneko said. In the holo, clusters of dots appeared in a rough circle about a third of the way down from the Cyrgal's prow.

"Guns, hold fire." Makarov tossed a data file into the tank and the projected course from the rogue wormhole appeared. She looked at the leading projected location and shook her head. "Too soon," she said. "If they're watching, then you just gave away the game."

Eight separate channels on one hailing frequency appeared in the tank.

Makarov opened the channel with a flick of her finger and stared at the Kul Rui Gassla kindred.

"What will happen if we engage a lepton pulse?" the veiled Cyrgal asked. Makarov glanced at the blue—friendly—icon closing on Ouranos. It was close enough that the *Concord of Might* couldn't intercept it now. How the faction on the surface might react was a harder question to answer.

"It will disrupt any cloaking shrouds it encounters," Makarov said. "Karigole technology isn't widely used, but if my suspicions are wrong, then we can all breathe a little easier."

Especially since you can't stymie my Armor's ticket off that planet anymore, she thought.

"The Karigole are a threatened species," said one of the kindred. "They've renounced space flight and have regressed to a tribal society. Why would they come here?"

"It's not the Karigole." Makarov sighed. "It's someone with Karigole technology."

"Admiral," Andere said, swallowing hard, "there's something on sensors."

Makarov looked to the course projection from the rogue wormhole, but there was nothing new. The XO swiped a hand across a screen and the tank zoomed in toward Ouranos. A long, jagged shape coalesced over the southern oceans in low orbit.

"No…" Makarov felt the blood drain from her face. "How could they be that fast?"

She touched the new contact and a Toth dreadnought—the

Last Light— appeared in the holo tank. The ship was irregular but resembled a battered spear tip, while the surface looked like an enormous coral reef had launched into the void. At almost twenty miles long and five miles wide, it dwarfed the *Warsaw* and the Cyrgal ship. Makarov noted cannon emplacements made of crystals the size of houses and watched as dozens of smaller contacts poured out from the bottom of the ship and streaked toward Ouranos and the Aeon's island.

"What is this?" asked one of the kindred.

"The Toth are here," Makarov said. "And they're here for the Aeon. That's the only explanation."

"This can't be," the veiled Cyrgal said. "There's been no contact with the Toth since…since…"

"They are here now!" Makarov shouted. That humanity had wiped all life off the Toth home world as part of the pact with a Qa'Resh entity and to bring an end to the Ember War was not a detail she needed to share with the Cyrgal. "That is a Toth dreadnought. My mother faced one during their incursion against Earth years ago. Their ships are resilient, armed with energy cannons that can—"

"We must attend a committee hearing," the cyborg said and the kindred's screens snapped off.

"They have to discuss this?" Andere asked, an eyebrow raised.

"Rail cannons ready to lay on target!" Eneko shouted across the bridge.

"Hold," Makarov said.

"Admiral, the longer we wait, the—"

"The Toth aren't stupid, guns." Makarov opened a menu in the holo tank and a cone extended from the Ibarra fleet toward the *Last Light*. The cone touched Ouranos's oceans and a coastline far from the Aeon's island.

"If our rail shot misses, it'll hit the planet," Makarov said.

"The almost completely *uninhabited* planet," Eneko said.

"Doesn't matter." Makarov swiped a finger down a screen and opened a channel to her wing commander. The head and shoulders of a woman in a void flight suit appeared in the holo tank.

"Admiral," the pilot said, "my Shrikes haven't fought Toth dagger fighters before…there will be a steep learning curve."

"Get Raptor bombers armed with cap-ship missiles void ready," the admiral said. "We're in for a fight."

The kindred reappeared.

"Ibarra ship," the cyborg said, "your presence has been granted a temporary acceptance, with conditions. You must join in the efforts to safeguard the Aeon."

"Certainly," Makarov said. "I can have rounds in the void in—"

"And you must not endanger the Aeon in any way. Violation of either provision will result in your immediate designation as a hostile presence."

"I don't have a clean shot at the Toth," Makarov said. "I can maneuver to assist, but if you want a guarantee we won't pound Ouranos dirt or water, it'll take us time to get into the fight."

"The Toth have refused our hails," said a Cyrgal female with a large jewel stud between her eyes. "Rudeness will not be tolerated. Please sign this joint action agreement."

A form that stretched from the top to the bottom of the holo projection appeared in the tank. Makarov swiped a hand to scroll up and text flew by. She swiped again. And again.

"You know what?" Makarov asked. "I won't shoot Cyrgal and Cyrgal won't shoot us. Agreed?"

"That is the essence of what is proposed," the jeweled alien said.

Makarov flung the agreement off to the side with a flick of her wrist.

"We'll shake on it later," Makarov said. "Earth got a good look at wrecked Toth ships after my mother beat the snot out of them. That fight was a while back. I don't know if the Toth have changed much since, but I'll send over technical readouts now."

Makarov glanced at the blue icon still on approach to Ouranos. The cloaked Destrier lander was still on the way, still hidden. The Armor's ticket off the planet was vulnerable, but protected for now.

Hurry up and get the Aeon out of there, Martel, she thought.

Chapter 15

Trinia came out of the jungle and went to the narrow channel separating the two islands. A group of nine Cyrgal stood on the other beach. The males had the double set of arms and carried plasma rifles; the three females had no augmentations

The Cyrgal went to their knees and kowtowed as Trinia approached.

Marc was a step away from leaving the jungle when Roland grabbed him by the shoulder.

"Stop," the Armor said. "Don't risk it. Those plasma weapons don't tickle."

"This whole thing will be a lot easier if I can convince the Cyrgal to stop being assholes about us being here," Marc said, trying to shrug off Roland's grip and failing. "You mind?"

"Hit the deck if things go wrong," the Armor said. "My mission's to bring her back safely." He let him go.

"I didn't think it was possible to like you even less, but here we are." Marc ran after Trinia.

The Cyrgal didn't react as he caught up with the Aeon.

"What's the plan?" he asked.

"You stay silent while I convince them to let you leave," she said.

"Are you their prisoner? The Ibarra Nation knows a thing or three about jailbreaks—loud, messy jailbreaks."

"You are no different than when we spoke through the probes." She shook her head.

Trinia stopped just short of the waterline. She spoke in Cyrgal and it took a moment for the box on Marc's wrist to translate.

"Tan-Mi, this isn't necessary," she said, loud enough for her voice to carry across the ten yards of water. "Return home."

"Mother of All," said a Cyrgal female as she pushed up from her bow, "your holy place has been disturbed. Let us cleanse it of the impure."

"What did they call you?" Marc asked.

"Silence," she hissed at him, then raised her voice. "Tainted flesh has not crossed the threshold."

She knocked on the top of Marc's head, sending a ring across the water. The rest of the Cyrgal got back to their feet, lowering the barrels of their plasma weapons toward the sand.

"The sanctity is preserved?" a male asked.

"As ever," Trinia said. "Do not attack the walkers. They will not attack you. This is my wish."

The Cyrgal went to their knees and bowed again.

"I can't stand it when they do that," she muttered.

"Let me talk to them." Marc raised a hand but Trinia pushed it back down, a grimace across her face as the cold bit into her flesh. She used her other hand to turn him around and push him back to Roland.

"You have nothing to say to them. Tell your soldiers not to fight them. Understand?" she asked as they walked together, Marc struggling to keep up with her longer stride.

"I can tell them that." Marc shrugged. "You can tell the big murder machines that too. See how that works out for you."

"You put savages in those weapons?" she asked.

"There's no such thing as a dangerous weapon," Marc said, "only dangerous people. Would be a waste to put a shrinking violet in there."

Roland had his helm angled up toward the volcano's flank.

"You saw aliens and you didn't kill any." Marc gave Roland a thumbs-up. "Knew you had it in you."

"There's something strange happening at the crash site," Roland said.

"Can you show us?" Trinia asked.

Roland did a double take at her, then extended a hand to the ground. The holo projector on Marc's wrist came to life.

Within the projection, the Cyrgal aircraft was wedged against a crevice running up the volcano's flank. The wings were broken, its spine cracked, and smoke seeped through the hull. A line of Cyrgal bodies lay on a field of rocks next to the crash and above the tree line. Three groups of Cyrgal stood in bunches while a single alien went from body to body. The loner wore a flight suit marred by fire, one arm secured to its side and covered by blood-soaked bandages. The wounded alien put his good hand under the neck of a dead Cyrgal, lifted it slightly, then went to the next body.

"Tragic," Trinia said. "Better if they'd all died in the crash."

"What is this?" Roland asked.

"Cyrgal kindred give birth at once. Between six and nine in a litter," she said. "They're almost inseparable after that. They learn together. Work together. Fight together. No Cyrgal ever does a thing alone. Ever. Litters won't breed until they've bought the right to marry into a clan. Then the bonded groups form a kindred. Most Cyrgal buy their way in through military service or labor work. When there are casualties or an accident that kills all but one of a litter…"

The lone Cyrgal stepped back from the dead and touched a hand to his forehead.

"The survivor is *xeren*. Alone. Not part of the fundamental group of their society. The survivor will never be allowed to form a kindred and they become pariahs," Trinia said.

The lone Cyrgal went to his knees and bent forward, holding his head straight from his shoulders.

A pair of Cyrgal males from a group flanked the kneeler and drew short swords from scabbards at their waists. They both set the blades to the survivor's neck.

"Wait," Marc said, "they're not going to—"

The Cyrgal raised their blades together and beheaded the survivor with matched strokes.

"Oh," Marc said faintly.

"Now they'll gather up the bodies and take them back for recycling," Trinia said. "Do we need to see that?"

The holo switched off.

"A waste," Roland said and escorted Trinia and Marc back through the jungle.

"You never learn to appreciate another culture?" Trinia asked him.

"Their business is their own, but that doesn't mean I have to agree with it," Roland said.

"And what would humans do with someone society cannot utilize?" she asked.

"We had—" Marc started.

Trinia shushed him.

"'Society' implies a desire to be a part of something greater than oneself," Roland said. "Hermits self-select out of interaction.

The individual can always contribute."

"That is how humans and Cyrgal will differ," Trinia said. "The group is everything for them. They are individuals that refuse to act as such. Lone action is forbidden. Consensus must reign."

"How do they ever make decisions outside their own groups without a leader?" Roland asked.

"Smart." Trinia touched two fingertips to her temple. "They are a fractured people. Divided up into thousands and thousands of clans that agree on nothing and never act as one…unless they're threatened. Once they recognize the whole is in danger, they cooperate. They united when they learned of the Xaros threat and managed to settle several worlds…though their colonies soon fell to civil war and nearly failed. The threat of local extinction put an end to the fighting once all sides were barely able to keep going."

"Religion doesn't do it for the Cyrgal?" Marc asked. "What was that 'mother of all' business."

"Ugh…" Trinia wiped a strand of sweat-logged hair from her face. "Ancient and very inconvenient myth. A female deity was alone on her mountaintop and decided to bless their home world with the first Cyrgal litter. When they found me, it triggered some old memories and a few kindred drew the unfounded conclusion. They tried to convince the rest of the settlers and a disagreement ensued. Clans fractured and the Tan Sar took up residence on the southern island and declared my hut sacred ground. The Kul Rui Gasslan is still negotiating with them. I'll die of old age before they come to a conclusion."

"And I thought old Earth governments were a pain," Marc said.

"Didn't take us long to have our own falling out after the Ember War," Roland said.

"There's still hope for a united humanity," Marc said, "but not while the Union has a death sentence on most of the Nation."

"What?" Trinia asked.

"There was this kid named Hale," Marc said. "Not the best guy to negotiate a treaty…"

****

The three returned to the silent village and Roland's IR came alive as the rest of his lance connected to his Armor through IR lasers.

Nicodemus, Martel and Morrigan stood guard around Trinia's hut.

"Sir." Roland saluted Martel with a fist to his chest.

"Water landings…not the best way to arrive," the colonel said and returned the salute. A dead fish slipped out from between Armor plates and flopped to the ground. "It's good you and the Nisei used the thumpers to contact us. Someone was heading out to deep sea."

"I got turned around is all," Morrigan said.

"You going to drag me away if I don't go peacefully?" Trinia asked Marc.

"We need your help," Marc said. "We won't force you."

"Then get off my island. Let me die in peace," she said.

On Roland's HUD, he saw a private channel open between Martel and Marc. The silver man's surface rippled as he spoke with the lance commander.

Trinia went to Martel and knocked on his breastplate. "You're the head man, yes?" she asked. "I wish to examine one of you."

Ripples emanated down Marc's arm to the wristband.

"Noninvasive, I promise," she said.

"Roland." Martel pointed at him, then to Trinia.

In his womb, Roland grit his teeth. First nursemaid for Marc Ibarra, now this. He was the junior lancer and would always be first for any extra duty that came up until he was promoted ahead of the rest of his lance mates or they were replaced with a junior soldier. The former was likely impossible, given how long the other three had their plugs, and he never wanted the latter to come to pass through death or injury.

"Sir," Roland said.

Trinia motioned for Roland to follow and gave Marc a dirty look as he tagged along. She went to the long building across from the unfinished triptych. Roland ducked inside and watched as she struggled to lift a door hidden in the floor of the space. Ornate, wrought-metal chairs along the walls were the only other feature.

Roland grabbed the door edge and lifted it up. The middle of the thick hatch was a silver metal that glinted like a geode.

"Quadrium," Marc said. "The Xaros drones couldn't scan through it. Kept them from ever finding my secret facilities in

Phoenix and a few bolt holes across the solar system."

Stairs led down a wide, winding tunnel.

"Come." Trinia hiked up her tunic and hurried down the steps. Roland struggled with the oddly sized steps, designed for the taller Aeon and not to scale for his Armor...or for Marc.

"I'm like a toddler sneaking into a basement," Marc said.

Roland continued down and activated a floodlight inside a hatch on his left shoulder for the shorter man's benefit. The staircase ended in a room the size of the briefing hall on the *Warsaw*, the ceiling polished rock, the walls lined with Aeon equipment. A sliver of glass floated over a dais in the middle of the room.

"Your probe." Marc peered up at the sliver, his fingers rubbing against each other as he fought back the urge to touch it.

"Dead," Trinia said. "It self-destructed the moment I returned during the Xaros attack on Bastion. Just a hunk of crystalline material now."

"Mine switched off after the last Qa'Resh wished us well," Marc said. "We need one to help Stac—" He looked at Roland and caught himself. "It would be useful to have another. Is all."

Trinia opened a case and removed a wire gauntlet. She slipped it over one hand and the fingertips glowed to life.

"All my old equipment still works." She reached toward Roland and he took a step back.

"It's not like she's going to take your temperature the old-fashioned way," Marc said.

"Passive sensor," she said, touching the gauntlet, "won't interfere with your systems."

Roland locked his arms at his sides. Trinia came closer, and he got a good look at her. She was less humanlike than he first guessed. Tiny membranes fluctuated next to her eyelids and the strands of what he thought were vines wiggled slightly along her hairline.

"You're past puberty," she said as she made a circular motion over his chest with the gauntlet, "but not too far into adulthood. A number of contusions and abrasions…stem-cell treatments to one arm. Is the synaptic feedback from damage to your Armor so strong that your body manifests it as an injury?"

"I am Armor." He moved the foot on the plasma-scorched leg from side to side. She moved her hand lower and Roland swore he felt a tingle along his true leg.

"No such injury to that extremity…"

"I got hurt out of my Armor," Roland said.

"Why would you get into an altercation outside this." She moved behind Roland and swept her hand slowly across the upper housing of his suit's integration system with his womb.

"Not my choice. Some old friends and I…had a falling out."

"Marc shared a number of human stories with me while we worked together. Human male conflicts that are not fatal can sometimes resolve the dispute, true in your case?" she asked.

"No. Not in mine," Roland said. The image of Aignar lying on the prison floor, limbs damaged and prosthetic chin dangling open, made him sick to his stomach.

"The rework to your nervous system is…competent. Not as perfect as the directions I sent over." She gave Marc a look.

"The surgery is different for every soldier," Marc said. "The design you did on that baseline I sent you had to be adjusted for the individual. A long and expensive procedure."

"And there are still errors," Roland said.

"There is some variance to the template I worked off of,"

Trinia said, "but your functionality is acceptable. How do you guard against overloading your neural system? There are a number of buffers missing."

"You mean redlining?" Roland asked. "We push ourselves as close to the edge as we can without going over. Armor is not for the timid. Too many buffers and our performance degrades. Might as well go back to tanks with three or four crew if we're afraid to take that risk."

"Curious," she said.

"You think a will to win is curious?"

"No, there's a communication node in the suit-to-pod interface I've not seen before," she said. "I think it's some sort of quantum dot but I don't recognize—"

"New system evolution," Marc said quickly. "A backup to the IR processors. I thought you wanted to examine flesh and blood, not hardware."

"Can you come out?" she asked. "I…would like to see you in person."

"This mission isn't over," Roland said. "The only way out is an emergency flush, and if I do that, I won't be able to be this…"

he tapped his chest, "until I make it back to a maintenance bay. Death before dismount."

"There's that...are there children on Earth?" she asked.

"I showed you—" Marc objected, but stopped when she pointed a finger at him.

"There are," Roland said. "And on Navarre. And Proxima. And hundreds of other worlds."

"Then it really did work." She stripped the gauntlet off and tossed it into a dusty corner. "It could have worked for the Aeon."

"What happened wasn't your fault," Marc said.

"Of course it was," she snapped. "My design. My plan. My responsibility."

"Why are you the last?" Roland asked.

"OK, you are a test subject," Marc said. "Do me a favor and shut your trap. Or your speakers. Whatever."

"It is like you to keep secrets," Trinia said. "The mind is the soul. The body it inhabits is secondary."

"Just ignore him, Trinia," Marc said. "He doesn't need to know."

"Oh, but he does." Trinia wiped a tear away. "You know.

Does anyone else? What good is a partial legacy for the Aeon? A legend must be part warning, part ideal. Does human history work like this?"

"Stacey knows," Marc said. "How many of the others on Old Bastion…I have no idea."

"Then let me show you." A workstation flickered to life as she approached. A golden lattice appeared in the air over the station, Qa'Resh technology that Roland had seen Stacey using before.

The sound of moving gears rumbled through the laboratory.

"The plan to save humanity from the Xaros wasn't the first time Bastion had tried that idea," she said. "Marc recruited a fleet with a substantial military escort and sent it into a time skip just before the Xaros conquered your home world. That force was enough to retake the planet, then he used the procedural technology to rebuild your defenses and launch the final attack on the Xaros."

"If we weren't the first," Roland said, "then the other attempts must have failed."

"The Aeon had that honor." She turned toward the wall and

crossed her arms over her chest. "There is a finite supply of the quadrium used in the time-skip devices in any solar system. There was only so much, a limited volume that could be displaced long enough for the Xaros to pass through. We weren't willing to accept that the vast majority of our people had to be sacrificed to the Xaros to save a few. We...loved ourselves too dearly."

"Don't think the decision was easy for me," Marc said. "I struggled with that part of the plan for decades."

"You knew how I failed," she said. "Was that a factor in your final decision?"

"Of course."

"Then you were stronger than I and the rest of the Aeon," she said. "We had our chance to test our plan fully, but then we wouldn't have had enough quadrium to secure every last one of our people. To triage a million or more of us away...unthinkable."

"There were maybe a hundred thousand of us that escaped the Xaros invasion," Roland said. "I was just a kid at the time...but how many Aeon were there if you thought you could save them all?"

"Two and a half billion," Trinia said. "My plan—"

"Your entire people agreed to it, along with the Qa'Resh," Marc said.

"*My* plan was for the Aeon to transfer their minds into the probe," she said, giving the dead machine in the middle of the room a sidelong glance, "then into procedural computers. The minds would be transferred into new bodies once the Xaros drone armada was light-years away. But holding so much data ran the risk of degradation…corruption. So every storage bank would sidestep the wait."

"You…you did this to every Aeon?" Roland asked.

"It had to be total. If the Xaros found a single one of us alive, they would have scoured the entire planet clean like they almost did to Earth. If they found a dead planet, they would preserve everything. The Dotari returned to their home world in such a state. They are blessed. So all the Aeon left their bodies and put their minds into my trust," Trinia said. "My husband. My children. My parents. All of them.

"The process was complete decades before the Xaros were to arrive. Then we activated the time-skip devices and I returned to Bastion to wait until the Xaros had moved on and the Crucible was nearly complete."

The gears stopped with a thump that resonated through the laboratory. The rock walls slid up, and rows upon rows of procedural tanks, large enough for an Aeon, stretched out into the darkness beyond.

In each tank was a skeleton, lying in a heap of bones or leaning against the glass. Bits of stretched skin and tufts of hair were all that remained of flesh.

"My god, Trinia…" Marc looked away.

"The plan…failed." The Aeon went to the window and put a hand to the glass. "The time jump caused a malfunction in the storage banks. Every mind was corrupted. Scrambled. When I brought the first back to life, they…didn't survive long. A few were gibbering maniacs that couldn't walk or eat or even realize who they were.

"I tried to salvage a few," she said. "But the corruption got worse and within a few days it was pointless. This isn't the only rebirth facility. There are dozens more across the planet. The final tomb of the Aeon."

Roland looked across the endless rows of failed bodies, then to Marc Ibarra. Just what the man had gone through to avoid this same fate for humanity...he couldn't help but admire the strength of will such acts took.

"I was about to throw myself into the ocean when the probe convinced me to continue," she said, "that there was still a way the Aeon might return. It was enough. I came up with the procedural mind-generation system. The probe had enough of our history and culture stored that it could manage a passable Aeon...but there was a problem."

"No genetic ingredients," Marc said.

Trinia touched her stomach.

"We had half the equation," she said. "Male Aeon reach maturation through conscious control over their bodies...none of them survived to provide that for me and all the embryos in the tanks were already fertilized. I never planned for failure. I was so *sure* of my own perfection.

"So I returned to Bastion, reworked the gambit from the beginning, and we waited, searched for another species that could do what the Aeon couldn't...and possibly help me."

"Et voila." Marc tapped his chest. "The Ibarra Nation is

here."

"Help? Help how?" Roland asked.

"With the right gene editing we could create Aeon-human hybrids," Marc said.

"What?" Roland took a step toward Marc. "That's…that's—"

"Impossible," Trinia said. "The Qa'Resh and I worked toward that goal for years. The research was incomplete when the Xaros destroyed Bastion. All the work was lost."

"You agreed to this?" Roland asked Marc.

"Don't get all high and mighty on me," Marc said. "Stacey Ibarra is the product of genetic engineering. It was the only way she could transfer her mind through the probes to and from Bastion and be our ambassador. I did this to my own daughters. I'm not proud of that but it was necessary. We'll find volunteers to…help the Aeon."

"Don't bother," Trinia said. "It is a fool's errand."

"Not if we find the Ark," Marc said. "The work will begin again. The Aeon can return."

Trinia tapped a finger on the top of Marc's head. "It won't

be you," she said, then turned to Roland. "You're flesh and blood within that Armor. Would you volunteer to do it? Father a race of hybrids?"

"We…we've just met," Roland said.

"We have crèches all across Navarre with everything we'd ever need." Marc shot Roland a look, his eyes alive with anger. "You have my word, Trinia."

"Your word is one thing," the Aeon said, "but the rest of the galaxy would have a vote. Your procedurals are marked for death. If I bring forth more of my own people in the same way…"

"We will win the war," Marc said. "With the Ark it will—"

A series of thumps echoed through the laboratory.

"What the hell is that?" Marc asked.

"Morse code from thumpers." Roland raised his helm. "R-T-B. Return to base."

"What's wrong?" Trinia asked.

"It's just those three letters," Roland said. "Let's move."

The Aeon went to the central dais and a compartment opened. She took out a necklace made of crystal flakes and wrapped it around her hand.

"You want big boy to carry you up the stairs?" Marc asked Trinia. "He's a pro at hauling people around."

"I wish you'd never have come here," she said.

Chapter 16

Rain lashed against Santos's Armor as he walked through the storm. He was at the front of the loose formation, with Gideon and Aignar both a few dozen yards behind him and to either side. The IR systems could barely maintain coherency in the storm and Gideon had forbade any other radio transmissions for fear the Kesaht might detect them.

Even though he knew his lance mates were in the same storm, marching through the rain—which almost flew sideways with the wind gusts—was a solitary experience. His suit's inertial navigation system kept him on track to an occupied spaceport on the other side of a mountain range. While he could barely see more than a few yards with his standard optics, he likened the travel to driving down a road at night. Even with only headlights, one could get to where they needed to go so long as they stayed on the road.

"Santos," Gideon said to him on a private channel, the transmission laced with static from moisture interference.

"On point, nothing significant to report," Santos said.

"Heard. Where were you during the recent…incident on Mars?" the captain asked.

Santos looked over a shoulder to where Aignar's shadow lumbered through the rain. The other Armor wasn't part of this conversation and couldn't step in to keep him from stepping on his own tongue.

"Gunnery drills on Titan, sir," he replied. "There was a system-wide lockdown while the Ibarran incursion was underway."

"What did your cadre tell you about the Ibarrans?"

"That there was a jailbreak. Illegal Ibarran procedurals rescued—I mean, escaped—from some secret prison on Mars. Something about spies. Most of our maintenance crew had to go through naissance inspections. Blood tests to make sure they weren't Ibarran spies. They were not happy about that. The Naissance Act is pretty explicit about birth circumstances not being used against anyone."

"Such is the nature of the war we're in," Gideon said. "The Ibarras poisoned the minds of a number of Union citizens before they turned traitor. Used them as sleeper agents and then killed them once they weren't of any use. Disposable tools—that's all human beings are to the Ibarras."

"No argument there," Santos said. "Then...then there was the Templar in the same prison." He winced, readying for a sharp retort from his commander.

"And what of the Templar?" Gideon asked, a dangerous edge to his words.

"Traitors," Santos said quickly. "All of them. They refused to carry out the Omega Provision as ordered and defected to the Ibarras. One of my sister training lances had a Templar as a cadre, but she was recalled to Mars shortly before the incident."

"You understand that they're our enemies now. No matter what they did for the Union or who they used to be," Gideon said.

"Understood, sir," Santos said, though in his heart, he was less than convinced. Just how so many Armor could abandon the Union so quickly...there must have been more to the story than what he'd heard through official channels, but poking around for details did not strike him as a smart move.

"Good…good. Your father sent me a message," Gideon said.

"Oh no…" Santos half turned around to look at Gideon, but a knife-hand gesture from the captain put his focus back on the path in front of him. "I don't want any special treatment. I don't care what he said or what he promised. He's not—"

"Diego Orozco is a hero of the Ember War," Gideon said. "I fought beside him, briefly, against the Toth."

"You were on Hawaii?"

"I'll show you a memento when we dismount," Gideon said. "Would you like to see the message?"

Santos felt emotions roiling in his chest. He knew every second he hesitated before answering was an admission that his father's message did matter to him, and such emotions were weakness for Armor.

"Sir. I don't think that—contact!" Santos braced his feet against the ground and aimed his rotary gun and gauss cannons as a form stumbled through the storm.

"Hold fire," Gideon said.

Santos tracked the humanoid shape as it stumbled through the rain, barely tall enough to reach the top of his Armor's thigh, its head and shoulders covered by a dark cloth against the rain.

Gideon approached, his boots splashing in puddles. The sound traveled through the storm and the figure's head perked up.

A brutish Rakka stared down Santos's gun barrels. The alien took a step back, mouth puffing, rain flying off its lips like spittle.

"Kill it," Gideon said.

Santos took a step forward and swiped a hand down, snatching the Rakka by the leg and lifting it into the air. The alien snarled like an angry dog and swung at the Armor's wrist.

"Scans clean of any tech," Santos said. "Maybe it knows where the Risen is hiding."

"How'd it even end up out here?" Aignar asked. He traced a quick circle in the air and trotted away, then ran a perimeter around Santos and Gideon, spiraling outwards.

Santos lifted the Rakka higher, bringing its beady eyes level to his optics. The alien swiped a clawed hand covered in waterlogged hair at his helm and missed by almost a foot.

"It looks like a caveman and a bear mated," Santos said.

"It's intelligent enough to speak, isn't it?"

"You're wasting time. Kill it," Gideon said as he turned around slowly, scanning their surroundings.

The Rakka reached into its cloak and pulled out a serrated knife with a bone handle. Santos almost chuckled; the crude weapon couldn't hurt him.

"Rakka vil aror!" The alien gripped the blade with both hands and swung it over its head.

Santos reached out and caught it by the wrists before it could plunge the blade into its own chest. He twisted the knife out of the alien's hands and let it fall to the ground.

"Sir…it's a prisoner, correct?" Santos asked.

"Kesaht are never taken prisoner," the captain said. "When their ships are disabled, they purge their air and die. Rakka commit suicide when cut off from their Sanheel officers. You saw what that one just tried to do."

"This could be progress," Santos said. "A live specimen to interrogate. Study."

The Rakka began hooting and beating its fists against its head.

"Stop," Santos broadcast through his speakers and wrapped his hands around its arms, pinning them to its side. He turned the alien right side up.

The hooting grew louder and longer. His audio receptors picked up an infrasonic, low-frequency noise that could travel several kilometers through the ground.

"It's giving away our position," Gideon said evenly.

Santos squeezed slightly, compressing the Rakka enough to stop its diaphragm and lungs from functioning.

"Silence," Santos said, pulling up translation software, but none of the Kesaht languages were listed. "Some of you speak English. Can you understand me?"

He shifted his grip on the alien and its coat fell open. A necklace made of twisted leather swung against his thumb. Totems of carved bone rattled on the line. Two matted clumps of hair—one long and black, the other blond curls—flopped against each other. As one twisted around, Santos saw skin stained pink with blood.

Scalps. Human scalps.

Santos's grip tightened and the Rakka squirmed. He

stopped, loosening his hold enough for it to breathe. The alien's chest heaved and its head snapped from one Armor to the other.

"If you let it go, it will give us away to the enemy," Gideon said. "We're behind their lines. They'll hunt us down and the Risen will survive. You know what's at stake here. Kill. It."

Santos zoomed in on the scalps and wondered what chance those two soldiers had when the Rakka came upon them.

He grabbed the alien by the ankles and bashed its skull against the rocks. Magenta blood seeped into the inches of water over the ground.

"There is no mercy in this war," Gideon said. "No quarter asked. None given."

"Why are they even fighting us?" Santos asked, dropping the body to the ground.

"The Ibarras want us to believe the Toth are controlling them," Gideon said. "Truth. Lie. Doesn't matter. That they are the Union's enemy is reason enough for me to kill them. We are Armor. We are fury."

"We will not fail," Santos said, looking to the distance as the rain lessened ever so slightly. "We should keep moving. Get to the target while the weather's still masking our movements."

Gideon's anchor spike tapped a quick rhythm against the rock. A reply vibrated against their feet a few seconds later.

"I'll take point," Gideon said. "Aignar will link up."

Santos fell behind his captain. He gave the dead Rakka a quick look before it was lost in the storm.

Chapter 17

The Iron Dragoons entered a forest of trees with smooth bark, trunks thick as a ground car, their tops lost to a low fog and the night sky. Wet creaks and groans reverberated through the air and Santos looked up and switched his optics. The heat image of the forest canopy made him stop in shock.

Branches were growing out of the trees, like tentacles reaching out of an animal.

"That's…something," Santos said.

"Focus, kid," Aignar said.

Santos switched back to his night-vision filters and closed formation with his lance, keeping a few meters between each suit as they worked through the forest.

"Storm like that," Aignar said, "doesn't pay to have

branches that can catch the wind."

A lizard the length of a human arm scurried up a trunk. It stopped and canted its head from side to side, regarding the Armor.

"You'd think all this metal would convince animals we're not food," Aignar said. "But let me tell you about these whales on Nimbus IV."

Gideon's helm snapped toward Aignar.

"Some other time. I'll tell you some other time."

A shroud of fog descended through the forest as the sound of trees branching out continued, squealing like a wet log in a firepit.

Gideon sent a map image to the lance. The three were on a mesa, a few hundred yards from the edge. A firing point with ID4—Santos's designation as the fourth-ranked Iron Dragoon—blinked at the top of the cliff.

"We'll have a clear shot on the supply depot from there," Gideon sent. "Priority targets are logistics transports, then container yards, then warfighting equipment. Santos, you understand why?"

"Desired effect is to draw the Risen out of his position on the front lines. If the Kesaht supply system can't get bullets and fuel to him, he has to go back to rearm," Santos said. "And any tanks or armored personnel carriers there are either in the depot for maintenance—and out of the fight—or fresh to the battlefield and will need all the supplies we're about to blow to hell."

"Sound analysis," Gideon said.

Santos felt a weight fall off his shoulders.

"Synchronize fire once you're anchored," Gideon said. "Break for your positions and avoid enemy contact."

"Moving," Santos said and took off at a run, following his HUD's path to the edge of the mesa. Gideon and Aignar split off in separate directions.

The pounding of his feet through the woods was oddly comforting. To run and not tire once struck him as a miracle of the technology. To fight without fatigue, without the limitations of his muscles and endurance, gave him a confidence that he'd never experienced before. In Armor, the only thing holding his performance back from the limit of the suit was the soldier's mind.

A rumble came through his audio receptors—pounding

footfalls at odds with his cadence. Neither Gideon nor Aignar were close enough to make IR contact in the fog. Santos slid to a stop next to a wide tree trunk and braced a shoulder against it. The rumbling grew louder and a herd of equine creatures with deep-purple skin bolted out of the forest and stormed past him.

The creatures' heads came up to the middle of his chest, enormous in size compared to an Earth horse. One of them reared away from Santos and crashed to the ground, tripping up two more of its kind.

The one on the ground let out a bleat and scrambled to its hooves. It bounded away.

"There a fire?" Santos wondered out loud. He stepped away from the tree and continued, his feet sinking slightly in the soil churned from the herd's passing.

He moved forward carefully. He had the least distance to cover to his firing point and could afford to be cautious.

A wet slap carried through the fog, followed by a clank of metal.

Santos unlocked his MEWS hilt from his thigh and keyed the blade into a short-bladed gladius configuration. Dew coalesced along the metal.

In a small depression between trees, the edges rimmed with thick roots, a Kesaht armor crouched over a dead equine lying in blood-soaked mud. The Kesaht's armor was filthy and bore crude runes dabbed in blood and ash on the shoulders and back. It ripped a handful of flesh away and stuffed it into its mouth. Needle-sharp teeth chewed, but the flesh just squeezed through the fleshless jaw and dribbled down the back of the mouth.

The Kesaht was feeding, but nothing went into the metal body.

Santos stopped at the edge of the depression, feeling a mixture of shock and disgust at what he saw. He flipped the gladius into a reverse grip and jumped toward the Kesaht, blade stabbing downward.

The alien swiped a claw through the air and deflected the strike, the edge drawing sparks as it nicked the Kesaht's forearm. The enemy's blood-soaked mouth opened and a roar burbled out of a speaker within.

Santos bashed the hilt against the Kesaht's head, turning the roar into a stream of static. The enemy grabbed him by his forearm, pushing the blade up and away, then raised a knee up to its chest and kicked Santos in the thigh, knocking the leg back and unbalancing him. It wrapped a hand around his sword grip and tried to pry it out of his hand.

Santos let it go and the gladius bounced off the equine's body and into the mud. The Kesaht shoved the Armor back and picked up the weapon.

Electricity crackled out of the hilt and up the Kesaht's arm. The alien's grip tightened as the discharge overloaded the Rakka's brain inside the suit.

Santos stomped a boot onto the Kesaht's foot and threw an uppercut into its midsection. The blow jerked it up, and its pinned foot kept it from going flying and transferred the force of the blow into its body.

The Kesaht tore free at the waist and flopped into the dirt. Santos lifted a heel and crushed its sternum with a crack of metal. Sparks spat out of the throat speaker like a last dying breath.

He grabbed the edge of the hilt and the electric storm shut off.

"That's mine," he said, slapping the flat of the blade against a knee to knock blood and bits of mud away.

The rumble of an oncoming stampede sounded through the fog. He looked toward the rim and dropped into a defensive stance as two more Kesaht armor came charging at him. One leaped forward, claws out and reaching for him.

Santos drove a knee up and into the Kesaht's chin, breaking teeth into a shower of glinting metal. The Kesaht's momentum carried it forward and it managed to get its arms around Santos. The two fell to the ground with a thump.

Santos passed the gladius to his other hand and pressed his fist against the side of the Kesaht's neck as its legs tried to wrap around him and lock him in place. The fist retracted and a punch spike shot into the alien's neck, cracking joints and servos.

The other Kesaht stood over them and raised its hands, then swung the clawed tips of its fingers at Santos's helm.

The Armor wrenched the punch spike inside the neck housing and ripped off the Kesaht's helm. The other enemy's strike shredded the helm into a thousand pieces. Santos squeezed the hilt on his gladius hard and the blade morphed into a thin cone with a sharp point. He drove the point into the other Kesaht's knee servo, jamming it into place.

Santos then shoved the headless enemy off him and rolled to one knee.

The Kesaht beat at the weapon lodged in its knee, snarling as it sent a jolt through its hands every time it touched it.

Santos yanked out the gladius and stabbed it into the Kesaht's chest, driving the spike up to the hilt. The Kesaht froze as though it had been shut off, and Santos drove a shoulder into it, using the blow to free his weapon.

The headless Kesaht kicked and beat in the mud. Santos stood over it, pinned a flopping arm to the ground, and rammed the spike into the brain case. He slid it out and looked back at the half-eaten creature, then to the Kesaht at his feet.

"What was done to you?" he asked. "Do the ones that locked your mind in there even know what you're going through? They even care?"

With a flick of his wrist, he drew the spike back into the hilt and locked it onto his thigh just as an alert flashed on his HUD. The fire mission was less than five minutes away.

Santos cursed and took off at a run, pushing his Armor as

fast as it would go, heedless of the noise he was making.

The forest thinned and he came out into a small clearing that ended with a steep drop into a gray abyss of fog. He slid to a stop with a shower of small rocks.

As Santos changed his optics to infrared, the valley beneath the fog came into view and he saw a sprawling spaceport ten kilometers away. He recognized the design of quick-built Terran Union warehouse domes and prefabricated buildings. Circling the spaceport was a sprawl of geodesic huts, cut through with wide avenues leading into the port. A massive Kesaht lander—a squat, ugly ship with a hull that looked like it was made of segments of tree bark nailed to the ship's frame—took up most of the main pad.

A low defensive wall formed the inner perimeter and Santos spotted weapon nodes every few hundred yards. The Union kept rail guns inside; what the Kesaht had replaced the weapons with was not a question he wanted an answer to just yet.

"New guy," Aignar's voice came through the IR, weak and static-laden. "Drop your damn anchor. Manual aim."

"Manual? At this distance?" Santos lifted a foot and a drill bit extended out of his heel. He rammed it into the ground and it bore into the rock beneath the topsoil. He opened the rail vane housing on his back and extended the twin matte-black lengths over his shoulder and aimed it at the spaceport in the distance.

Energy flooded the magnetic capacitors and he unsnapped a shell the length of his Armor's hand off his waist. He tapped the shell against his helm twice and snapped it into the rail gun's breech.

"You didn't see the sensor globes they've got on the walls?" Aignar asked. "You use a targeting laser, they'll backtrack it instantly. You want to eat counterfire?"

"I just got here," Santos said, watching as the charge level on the rail gun ticked higher. "Ran into some trouble."

"Santos, your target is the ship," Gideon said.

"Confirmed," he said. Bringing the crosshairs onto the alien lander, which was nearly the size of a Union cruiser, he realized the captain had given him the largest, easiest-to-hit target.

"Base activity picking up," Aignar said. "Got Sanheel running around their motor pool."

"They know we're out here," Gideon said.

"I took them down without firing a shot," Santos said.

"But…no excuse, sir. They must have sent back a warning."

"Thirty seconds from now, they'll know exactly where we are," Aignar said.

Santos cut the input from his audio receptors and braced himself against the inside of his pod. Rail cannon shots had the advantage of firing a hypervelocity slug that traveled with enough velocity to make orbit meant that correcting for wind and other gunnery factors to a short range target was an afterthought. The blast wave from such a shot, on the other hand, was of significant concern.

Rail guns were meant to be fired in a vacuum. Employing them in an atmosphere would be deadly to any unarmored living thing nearby.

"On my mark," Gideon said.

Santos stared at the enemy ship. His heart skipped a beat when hull segments snapped open and point defense turrets came out.

"Sir, they've got—"

"Fire!" Gideon ordered.

Santos delayed just long enough to feel the slap of twin blasts of overpressure against his Armor. He dragged his crosshairs onto the lander and fired. Lightning arced down his vanes and the shell launched, leaving a trail of ignited oxygen in its wake.

The lander buckled like it had been stuck by an invisible axe. The forward section broke away and crashed to the ground and fire exploded out of the point defense turrets.

"Ha! Direct hit!" Santos shouted.

There was a rumble beneath his feet. He looked down and a crack opened in the ground from his anchor and spread to the cliff's edge.

"Crap." He began unscrewing his anchor from the bedrock, but he was still locked to the ground as the ground beneath his feet collapsed into a small depression. He heard the rumble of boulders breaking loose and falling into the valley.

The ground between him and the cliff edge sloped down and slid away.

"Crap. Crap!" His anchor came loose and he backpedaled, his heels digging into the soil as it loosened into a stream of dirt pouring over the cliff. Santos launched himself backwards and rolled over. He crawled through the collapsing ground, trying to reach the nearest tree, but it felt like he was swimming against a river.

He sank into the growing avalanche, and just as it occurred to him that his father wouldn't even have a body to bury, something clamped onto his arm and the roar of dirt subsided.

He looked up at Aignar, dangling in the air above him. One hand grasped Santos's forearm; the other held on to Gideon's foot. The captain had his arms wrapped around a tree trunk, and his fingers dug into the bark.

Santos looked down to a long drop into a cloud of pulverized rock.

"You waiting for an engraved invitation?" Aignar asked. "Climb, bean head!"

Santos reached up and clamped on to Aignar's upper arm. He used his lance mate as a field-expedient ladder to get up to Gideon and onto the new edge of the cliff.

Aignar followed him, scrambling over the edge and hugging the ground.

"Nice terra firma. Sweet terra firma," he said, patting a patch of grass.

As a messenger drone shot out of Gideon's mortar and streaked into the sky, Santos looked back at the spaceport. The lander was engulfed in flames, the inferno spreading to nearby supply yards. Small explosions rippled through the valley.

"You're the only one that got a hit." Aignar bopped Santos on the helm. "Point defense came online just before we fired and took out our shots. Why didn't you say something?"

"I did! That's why I staggered my round." He tossed his hands up and dirt went flying. "Point defense intercepts the initial volley, but can't react fast enough to reorient to the next attack from a different vector. Funny, that was my last lesson on Titan before I got yanked out of training."

"It was enough," Gideon said. "I sent a report to General Kendall. With all the confusion from the depot being hit, it should get through. Move out. We need to get to our own resupply."

Gideon helped the two to their feet and slapped Santos on the shoulder.

"Well done, Iron Dragoon," Gideon said and took off at a run.

Santos was caught flat-footed by the compliment and fell in behind Aignar.

In his pod, a smile spread across his face.

Chapter 18

Makarov watched as the Toth dreadnought flew over an icy archipelago on Ouranos's southern pole.

"Still don't have a clear shot," Eneko said.

In the holo, the *Concord of Might* bore down on the planet, the ponderous vessel pushing forward with all engines blazing. Dozens of new contacts emerged from the Cyrgal ship and sped ahead as a wire diagram of a Cyrgal gunship appeared in the holo tank.

"No fighters," Makarov said. "Their smallest ship has to carry a full kindred at once."

"Maybe they'll trade the lack of maneuverability for increased firepower," Andere said. "I would."

"Amazon," Makarov called her wing commander by her call

sign, "ready for IR launch."

The helmeted pilot appeared in the holo, her Shrike's cockpit surrounding her.

"*Roger,* Warsaw *actual,*" Amazon said. *"Know we're running the risk of degraded connection with the atmosphere and distance."*

"I'm aware," Makarov said. "Have self-destruct safeguards in effect. We make one screw-up, two giant ships will want our blood."

"No pressure," Amazon said and snapped off her channel.

"*Concord of Might,*" Makarov said, touching the Cyrgal ship, "cut your velocity twenty percent. My fleet is about to engage."

The cyborg alien appeared in the tank.

"Our ship must match the invader's orbital plane to fire on them with no threat to the Aeon," he said. "Our present vector will allow several minutes of sustained fire. While the dreadnought will be destroyed in close orbit to the planet, we've enough time to mitigate damage to Ouranos from debris."

"It's a big ship," Makarov deadpanned.

"We have every intention of blowing it into small pieces. Reentry friction will take care of the trash."

"I like the way you think," Makarov said. "Be advised the ship will be shielded and—"

"Not an issue for the amount of firepower we will bring to bear," the alien said.

"Toth shields have an oscillation period that can be exploited. Give my guns enough time to find it and—"

"The decision has been remanded to a committee." The Cyrgal cut the transmission.

"How I wish we were doing this with the Dotari," Makarov muttered. "They know how to get things done."

"Toth fighters are boosting," Andere said. In the tank, tiny icons sprinted ahead of the *Last Light* toward the Cyrgal ship. The fighters and gunships were on a collision course.

"The dreadnought that hit Earth carried three times as many fighters," Makarov said, crossing her arms and looking at Andere. "They keeping a reserve to throw at us or do they think they sent up enough to beat the gunships?"

"Toth weren't afraid of casualties," the XO said. "Neither are the Kesaht. Economy of force isn't one of their principles of war. If they had the fighters, they'd send them."

"Big *if*," Makarov said. "We don't know how many Toth survived the destruction of their home world. Those could be the last of their combat void fighters."

"They have plenty of Kesaht cannon fodder," Andere said. "Why send a Toth ship for this?"

"The galaxy doesn't know the Toth are behind the Kesaht," Makarov said. "Earth and the Lady aren't exactly eager to mention the Toth…begs a number of questions we don't want to answer. Plus, the only proof we have is a couple Toth warrior bodies left behind on Balmaseda…which isn't definitive. The overlord sent that ship to keep blame off the Kesaht."

"Does this change the operation?" Eneko called out.

"Negative." Makarov shook her head. "Let's see if we can poke the hornet's nest."

****

Commander Belasco heard the tick of her ventilation tubes as she breathed deeply within her flight helmet and looked up at the Raptor bombers flying just above her Shrike fighter. The larger craft flew perilously close to each other, nearly bumping stubby wings while in their void configuration.

Ahead, Ouranos hung in the void, deep blue oceans and a decent hurricane making up most of what she could see on the planet. The icon for the Toth dreadnought was a single pulsing, still-distant icon on the inside of her canopy. She could make out the pale-red glint of the ship's hull, just a sliver against the night.

An alert flashed on her HUD.

"Trident squadron, this is Amazon," she sent over the IR network between the Ibarran ships. "Rail cannons are laid. Slave the launch sequence to the *Warsaw*'s fire control and stand by."

"Think we'll get the Toth's attention?" asked her wingman, Garrote.

"Fighting Toth is in Makarov's blood," Belasco said as two Raptor squadrons sent ready signals through the IR. Glancing up, she saw weapon bays open across the bomber's underside. Launch rails bearing torpedoes snapped out of the internal bays.

"Bombardiers," Belasco said, tightening her grip on her control stick as a timer popped up on her HUD, "reminder to engage self-destruct protocols in the event you lose positive control of your munitions. Don't risk collateral damage to the Cyrgal or the planet."

"There's only *one* alien down there," Garrote said. "Big sky, little bullet. The chances of hurting him-her-it are—"

"Instructions from the admiral stand," the wing commander said. "Stand by to launch."

"Speaking of big sky, little bullet…" Garrote mumbled.

The timer hit zero, and less than a heartbeat later, silver flashes snapped around the Ibarra attack wing. Rail shots from the *Warsaw* and her fleet tore through the void, missing the fighters and bombers by scant meters. Belasco winced as the hypervelocity slugs shot past, finding little comfort in knowing that if the fleet gunners were off by a hairsbreadth, she wouldn't even realize she'd been hit as a poorly aimed shell atomized her fighter.

Raptors fired their torpedoes with a flash of electromagnetic coils, the weapons flying at a significantly slower speed than the rail cannon shots. The torpedoes' engines remained off as the munitions sped away.

Belasco watched as status reports trickled in from the bombers.

"*Warsaw*, this is Amazon," she sent back to the fleet. "Dumb fire complete. Bombardiers have tight IR lock on their fish. Passing rail shots should mask the launch, if the Toth were even paying attention."

"Roger, Amazon," Admiral Makarov sent. "*Stand by for attack guidance.*"

"Standing by," Belasco said and cut the transmission.

"We've got to keep closing on the enemy for the IR to hold, reduce command lag," Garrote said. "What're the chances the Toth'll decide to come out and play with us?"

"Don't know, but if they do, we'll teach them a painful lesson in just how much better Ibarra pilots are compared to those amateurs from the Terran Union," she said. "I don't think I'd mind a decent dogfight, especially if the torps can't get through the shields. Hate to go through all this trouble and have nothing to show for it."

"From your lips to Saint Kallen's ears," Garrote said.

Belasco tapped a fist against her chest and felt sweat seep into her flight suit as shields flared on the *Last Light*. The first rail shells had hit home.

****

In the holo tank, rail shells peppered the Toth dreadnought. Shields flared as energy waves rippled over the surface and swept toward the prow.

Makarov nibbled on the inside of her lip as more data poured in.

"She's rotating her shields," Makarov said. "We didn't see this tech during their incursion on Earth."

"That was decades ago," Andere said. "They must have learned a lesson from that loss."

"Guns, can you figure out the harmonics?" the admiral asked.

"With enough data," Eneko said. "If the shields were static, we could slip shells through the low points in the oscillation. But if they're rotating across several nodes, then it—"

"Comms, get me the Armor on the line," Makarov said. "See if they can manage a shot from dirtside with their rail systems."

"Armor report they are decisively engaged with a Toth assault," the lieutenant said. "Still want me to send the request?"

"Belay that." Makarov frowned. Everything was coming to a head at once, naturally. She wondered if the Cyrgal had their own equivalent to Murphy's Law. "Guns, keep firing. Find an opening through the Toth shields."

In the holo tank, engines along the *Concord of Might*'s hull flared, maneuvering it into an orbital path that would come perilously close to the Toth dreadnought.

She opened a channel to the ship and the Cyrgal with the cyborg eye appeared.

"The Toth vessel is heavily shielded," she said. "Our shells aren't having any effect, but we're working to find an opening. Our sensor data is degraded by distance. Can your ship—"

"We will crush them," the Cyrgal said. "There is no reason to worry. Cease your fire. Any damage we suffer at your hands will be returned a hundredfold." The channel closed.

"Now they're motivated," Andere muttered.

Makarov placed her hands behind her back as the icons for the Cyrgal gunships and Toth fighters closed in on each other.

The admiral opened a ship-wide channel. "All hands, the battle is joined. *Warszawo walcz.*"

****

Belasco maneuvered her Shrike fighter farther away from her wingman as the wing settled against the upper reaches of Ouranos's atmosphere. The exosphere wasn't thick enough to affect her fighter's maneuvers, but looking down to the planet a thousand kilometers below had her itching to reconfigure the Shrike to extend the wings waiting in the fuselage.

If I have to bail, at least I'll have something to land on…probably water, but that's better than floating Dutchman, she thought.

"Hostile fighters and the gunships about to make a pass," Garrote said.

Dots of explosions burst to life between the *Last Light* and the Cyrgal ship. She zoomed in on the action and her HUD put an overlay of the dogfight across her vision.

The Toth fighters were shaped like serrated daggers, each carrying a single Toth warrior that used all six limbs to pilot. Bolts of energy snapped out from the dagger fighters and tore into the gunships. The forward wedge of the Cyrgal were torn apart, shredded by the Toth's combined fire. Second and third echelons spread apart, but the gunships were almost glacially slow compared to the Toth.

Dagger fighters ripped through the Cyrgal, landing hits with ease.

Turrets on the gunships managed to take down a few of the Toth, and missiles corkscrewed out of the sides and tops of the gunships, chasing after dagger fighters.

Belasco grimaced as a Toth swept past the nose of a gunship, leading the pursuing missile into the Cyrgal's cockpit.

The mass of Toth fighters continued through the gunships on their way to the *Concord of Might*. The gunship formation lurched onward, bleeding air from perforated hulls and trailing debris from destroyed ships.

"The Toth are better than the Kesaht," Garrote said. "I'll give them that."

"Their electric countermeasures are poor," Belasco said. "Cyrgal missiles had a higher hit rate than their turrets."

A lance of dirty-yellow energy struck out from one of the detached hull sections of the *Concord of Might* and hit the prow of the dreadnought. The beam broke against the shields and electricity arced against the inside of the shields like lightning crawling along the bottom of a storm cloud.

Belasco's HUD swam with static for a moment.

"By all that is holy," she said as she watched a hull section retract back into a Cyrgal ship and the edge of another glow to life.

"Amazon," Eneko came up on her HUD. "Enemy shields held, but there was a significant disruption to the harmonics during the strike. Need you to coordinate torpedo strikes with the lance hits."

"Are the Cyrgal sharing firing data?" she asked.

"Negative. We're asking, but they're not interested in sharing."

"My warheads are…ninety seconds out," she said. "We need a time on target to—"

Another lance of energy scoured across the top of the Toth ship and Belasco's ears filled with static.

"—well aware!" Eneko said. "Do what you can."

"Blast it." Belasco opened a channel to the Raptors. "Bombardiers, stagger warheads at ten-second intervals. Set to point detonation."

"Not sure how the shields will affect the IR controls," said one of the pilots. "If we set to PD and the torp goes rogue…"

"We're taking that risk. We're here to draw blood, not count coup," she said.

Small warning icons peppered around the Cyrgal ship as missiles streamed from launch tubes.

"Maybe they figured things out for themselves," Belasco muttered.

Giant crystals on the dreadnought's hull angled toward the Cyrgal ship. A torrent of blue teardrops of energy fire erupted, bolting through the void and annihilating what remained of the gunship formation, the Toth fire overtaking some of their own fighters before they could maneuver out of the way. Blasts struck the Cyrgal hull, leaving blackened craters around the apex of the cone.

"Lead warhead closing to final sprint," a bombardier sent.

"Hold for a Cyrgal strike," Belasco said. "Come on…come

on."

A hull section attached to the Cyrgal ship glowed bright...and exploded. Toth fighters danced along the ship's hull, targeting the thick power cables running from the main ship to the weapon sections.

"Not good," Belasco said. "Not good at all."

The *Last Light's* fire slackened, but focused on the Cyrgal weapon sections, knocking them out one at a time.

"Amazon," Eneko sent, "stand by for a mass fire strike on the enemy's stern. Set warheads to penetrate at 475-meter intervals from the target location."

A point blinked on the dreadnought's rear. Belasco extrapolated data and sent it to the bombers.

"Bombardiers, ready to sprint your fish in five...four..." Belasco caught her breath as rail shells slapped into the Toth shields.

"Balls, now! Sprint sprint sprint!"

Activated torpedoes came up in her display as the afterburners came to life, propelling them forward.

Belasco tapped knuckles to her heart and said a quick prayer to Saint Kallen as the torpedoes closed on the target.

Warheads exploded against the shields, but a handful made it through the disruption caused by the fleet's shelling.

"Lost contact!" a bombardier shouted. More crewmen echoed the call.

"Big ship. Don't miss," Belasco whispered.

A fireball erupted between a cluster of engine cones on the back of the dreadnought as a denethrite warhead struck home, exploding on contact. Another torpedo struck the base of a coral-like tower, snapping it off at the base and sending it cartwheeling against the hull. The segment shattered into pieces and swept forward like sand carried by the wind.

A handful of explosions flared among the engines and across the dorsal hull. The energy cannon fire tapered away to nothing.

Belasco punched a fist up next to her helmet.

"*Warsaw*, we've got effects on target," she sent back to the fleet.

On the Cyrgal ship, a pair of weapon sections glowed bright. One petered out, burning into a cinder. The other lashed out at the

Toth ship, the blow beating against the shields for a moment, then tearing through. The lance scoured across the dreadnought for a heartbeat, ripping apart cannons and blackening a scar against the hull.

The Toth warship rolled to one side, pushed by the Cyrgal strike.

"Ha ha! That got her!" Garrote shouted.

The Toth ship flipped over, exposing the bottom section to the Cyrgal. The other side of the Toth ship was undamaged and looked to be just as well armed as the other half.

The engine glow on the *Last Light* faded away.

"Raptors, prep rail cannon launch—" Belasco stopped as crystal cannons fired from the other side of the dreadnought, sweeping across the Cyrgal ship. Hull fragments were blasted loose, the few remaining weapon segments were destroyed, and the ship's cone skewed to one side as an internal explosion sent cracks through the ship's forward hull.

A pair of bolts slashed overhead and Belasco dove toward the planet. Three of her Raptors blinked red on her HUD. Destroyed.

"Amazon, this is Makarov," came from the *Warsaw*. "Break off your attack and make for an island along the southern coast. Sending the location now."

Belasco grunted as g-forces threatened to gray out her vision in the steep dive. A Toth bolt swiped past her nose, sending a buffet of turbulence through the thin air.

"Roger… *Warsaw*," she sent back.

Fire grew around her heat shields as her Shrike made for Ouranos's surface.

"Trident, make for this location," she said, sharing the location of the last Aeon with the rest of her wing as they followed her into the atmosphere. "Switch to atmo configuration soon as we hit chop."

Blue light from dissipating energy bolts splashed across her fuselage. A fireball erupted behind her and curses swept over the comms. Garrote's icon flashed red.

"Toth ship moving over the horizon," Eneko sent from the *Warsaw*. "Need you to make pickup and get the Aeon and the Armor back to the ship before they make an orbit."

"Heard," she said as she leveled out a few miles over the

ocean. Her fighter wobbled through the air like she was driving on an icy road until she extended the forward-sweeping wings and a rudder from her hull, stabilizing her flight.

"*Warsaw*, the Cyrgal going to finish off the Toth?" she asked.

"Doubtful. The *Concord of Might* is dead in space," Eneko said. "The fleet can't withstand the level of firepower the Toth still have. We need to leave this system soon as we have what we came for."

She glanced over the side to a string of tropical islands as a miles-wide murmuration of birds shifted against the coastline.

"Roger, *Warsaw*, we can get postcards some other time. Give me relay comms to the Destrier making the pickup."

Chapter 19

Roland emerged from the stairwell and his IR came to life with active channels.

"Fifteen landers to the east," Araki sent.

"Northern wave engaged by Cyrgal fighters. Total loss," Morrigan said.

"Templar four on the net," Roland said.

"Bring the principals to me at the hut," Martel said. *"The Warsaw wants to speak with them."*

He stepped out of the building and saw a battle raging in the twilight sky. Dagger-shaped fighters fought the larger, less maneuverable Cyrgal ships. Balls of fire streaked down, but slowed just before they struck the ocean. There was no outgoing or incoming fire from the island.

Roland hurried Marc and Trinia back toward the hut.

"What did we miss?" Roland asked.

"Toth," Nicodemus said as he ran over to join them.

Trinia slid to a stop, her face darkening from gold to bronze. "No…not them…" She backpedaled toward the long house.

"We'll protect you." Marc put his hands against the small of her back and she yelped with pain. "Sorry. Keep forgetting about the cold."

"Those are Toth fighters," Roland said. "No one's seen those since the Ember War ended."

"We can guess why they're here," Marc said to Trinia. "Let's go talk to the big cheese and figure out how to get you away from them, yeah?"

"This is your fault," Trinia said. "If you hadn't—"

"There's blame all over the place," Marc said, throwing his hands up. "We can wag fingers later. Problems to solve now, yeah?"

"You are infuriating!" she screamed.

"I get that a lot."

She looked up at the battle raging overhead, then ran to

where Martel and Morrigan stood by the hut.

"We're on the east flank," Nicodemus said. "Shore watch."

Roland nodded and followed the older Armor into the jungle, tearing through underbrush and wide fronds, startling flocks of birds.

"How bad is it?" Roland asked.

"*Warsaw* reported a dreadnought-sized vessel with support fleet. Not as big as what the Toth sent to Earth, but more than we can handle," Nicodemus said. "The Cyrgal on the moon are in committee. Everything you see in the air is from Tan Sar bases on the other island and the coast."

"Why aren't they landing on the island?" Roland asked.

"Did Gideon teach you nothing about the battle on Hawaii?" Nicodemus asked. "The Toth can swim—a hell of a lot better than we can. We're looking at an amphibious invasion."

"No Kesaht?" Roland turned his sensors to the sky, tagging passing landers.

"No…none of their landing vectors are coming close to this island. Why so much of a standoff?" Nicodemus asked.

They stopped at the edge of the beach and Roland took

cover behind a small copse of trees as he watched the water for emerging Toth warriors.

"They want her alive," Roland said. He gave Nicodemus a quick rundown on Trinia's role in creating the human procedurals and what he saw in the lab.

"The Toth came to Earth and demanded the tech to make their own proccies," Nicodemus said. "If Trinia was that vital to the program…then they could force her to create their own crèches."

"They'd create slaves. And food for the overlord," Roland said.

"We can't let that happen," Nicodemus said. "You understand what that means?"

Roland took a moment to grasp the implications. "She's the last of her kind, sir. We kill her and—"

"Save how many human lives from the Toth? I don't like it either. The best solution is to get her off world and back to Navarre with us," Nicodemus said. "We didn't come here to fail the Lady, did we?"

"Negative," Roland said.

Lightning flashed from a distant storm on the horizon, the clouds black and pregnant with rain.

"That's coming right for us," Roland said.

"It means nothing."

"Agreed. Nothing keeps us from the fight…Sir, do our Templar vows extend to human-alien hybrids?" Roland asked.

"What the hell did you do down there?"

"Nothing! Just a question that came up that's nagged at me."

"Focus on the practical problem we have," Nicodemus said, "such as how we defend the entire island with just us and the Nisei."

"Guile," Roland said. "I have an idea."

****

Thunder rolled over the beach as curtains of rain dimmed the setting sun and forks of lightning skittered across the bottom of the dark clouds. Roland watched the approaching storm front, thinking back to his un-armored battle on Mars and just how difficult it was to fight in smoke and through pain of wounds. He developed a great deal of respect for legionnaires and Rangers that day, though he would always call them "crunchies."

"Hostile air inbound," Nicodemus said. "Nisei have eyes on them from the west."

"Engage?" Roland looked back to the other side of the island.

"This was your plan. What do you think?" The other Armor shifted his Mauser heavy rifle up and braced it against a tree, muzzle toward the ocean.

"We'll know if they make positive identification soon enough, if the Cyrgal manage not to shoot this one down." Roland touched the magazine in his own Mauser, checking again that it was loaded firmly.

"They aren't the best listeners," Nicodemus said. "Even when the instructions come from the—what did they call her?"

"Mother of All. I can't say how much restraint they're really exercising right now, given our lack of training in alien theology. I just hope they play their part when it matters," Roland said.

"Principal in the open," Martel sent over the IR.

Roland's receptors picked up the whine of Toth engines and

his targeting systems triangulated the dagger-shaped fighter's location and projected course. The fighter banked over the pathway leading down from the Aeon village to the narrow strip of water between the islands. It slowed, making an easy, tempting target.

"Gauss or Mauser?" Roland asked.

"Make a statement," Nicodemus said.

"Mauser," Roland said and lifted the rifle to his shoulder as the Toth fighter accelerated. He pulled the trigger and magnetic accelerators launched a shell the size of a football. The fighter exploded into flames and debris rained down on the beach, hitting the sand with a sizzle.

"You think they took the bait?" Nicodemus asked.

Roland pulled back from the tree line and rushed to another firing position as he racked the charging handle on his Mauser to load another shell into the breach. Reloading the weapon like that, like it was some sort of antique from early twentieth-century warfare, felt like an anachronism, but the stress each shot put on the weapon was detrimental to anything as delicate as an autoloader system. A normal human couldn't even lift the weapon, much less survive firing it.

"We'll know in a second...contact." Roland marked dark spots in the ocean and sent the targeting information to the rest of the Armor. Threat icons appeared on his HUD from the other side of the island, all converging toward the channel.

Roland spotted a lizard-like head peek up between waves and fought the urge to open fire.

"Not yet," Nicodemus said. "They need to commit."

Behind him, he heard the sound of Morrigan and the colonel stomping down the pathway. He activated an optic on the back of his helm and saw Trinia through the trees, struggling to keep up with the Armor.

A ten-foot-tall wave reared up from the ocean, the wall full of dark blotches, each a Toth warrior.

"Here we go," Nicodemus said as the wave crashed against the beach.

Toth in crystalline armor, wielding halberds tipped with energy weapons, spilled out of the wave with an almost fluid grace. Their battle ululation sent a chill through Roland's body. A dozen had arrived with the wave, and the next whitecap building in the sea carried even more.

The warriors galloped forward on four legs, each ending with obsidian-tipped claws. For creatures so large, they moved with unnerving speed.

"Weapons free," Nicodemus said.

Roland fired his Mauser, obliterating a Toth and punching up a cloud of sand that enveloped a pair of the attackers.

Nicodemus' shot blasted a warrior in half and knocked a second off its feet. The report of Nisei Mausers from the other side of the island echoed around them.

"Mortars. Fire plan Bravo," Nicodemus said.

Roland racked his weapon and fired from the hip, killing a Toth, the force of the round's impact in the sand tripping up a second. He raised an arm and smashed through the trunks of a pair of trees, clearing the air above him as they fell.

A shell soared out of the tube on his back. The variable launcher in his Armor kept pumping rounds into the air. A blue bolt of plasma streaked out of the surf and just missed his shoulder, igniting a bush into a torch. Roland held his ground until his HUD signaled rounds complete.

Not a single shell had landed on the beach...yet.

Roland dove to one side as three plasma bolts converged on his old position. He rolled to one knee and put a double shot from his gauss cannons into a charging warrior's chest. Crystal shattered and sprayed out, mixed with yellow blood. The warrior pitched forward and landed face-first in the sand, sliding to a dead stop.

Dozens more Toth emerged from the ocean, all keening their battle cry.

It was then that the mortars struck. Using a launch force for each shell, the Armor brought every munition into the fight as one. Half impacted in the surf, sending up geysers and blasting a shockwave through the water that crushed Toth to death. The other half exploded seven yards over the beach, sending showers of shrapnel into those that had made it to shore.

The ululations died away with the passing explosions.

Roland shot a Toth crawling through the sand, watching as its yellow blood drained into the ocean. Dead Toth rolled ashore with the next wave, their armor riven with cracks.

"Lazy way to fish," Nicodemus said. "Fall back to the channel."

"Moving." Roland fired his Mauser into a Toth in a distant wave, blasting a gap in the wall of water and sending tiny bits of the warrior flying out the back. He ran through the jungle as plasma bolts stabbed out at him from the ocean.

"Need targeting data," Araki sent over the IR.

Roland queued a recon drone to launch out of his mortar, but got an error message on his HUD.

"Tube's too hot." Roland reached around and a drone popped out of a housing and into his hand. He chucked it into the air and quad rotors popped out of the drone as it cleared the jungle canopy and then zipped into the sky.

A green plasma bolt burst through a tree trunk and sent a shower of sparks over Roland.

"The Cyrgal are firing from the other island," Roland said into the IR net. "Who has positive comms with those idiots?"

"Principal's coordinating," Murayama, the fourth Nisei, sent. "You probably look like a Toth to them through all that jungle."

"Tell them to cease fire!" Roland rolled to one side and into a patch of sand as a Cyrgal bolt snapped past his head. "They need to fall back!"

A ripple in the jungle air moved toward him.

Roland brought his Mauser up and braced it overhead as a Toth halberd materialized and bit into the weapon. The Mauser bent, pinning the blade inside it. Roland twisted the wrecked weapon aside, yanked the partially cloaked Toth warrior off its feet, then dropped a shoulder and sprang forward. The blow pinned the Toth against a tree and the cloak dissipated.

Roland retracted a fist into his forearm housing and rammed a punch spike into the Toth. Armor cracked and the Toth clawed at Roland's shoulders and helm. He stabbed it twice more then pushed the limp body away.

His Mauser lay on the ground, broken in half and smoking. He gave the fallen weapon a quick salute and continued toward the channel.

"Got cloakers in the jungle," Roland sent through the IR.

"Roger," Nicodemus sent and an icon popped up on his HUD's map. *"Link up here."*

A flurry of Cyrgal plasma bolts erupted through the jungle to Roland's left as a tree blew free from its roots and slammed across Roland's waist, taking him off his feet.

"Tell...those idiots..." Roland gripped the tree's bark and sent splinters flying out from where his fingers met the wood. "To stop shooting at me!"

He thrust the trunk away and it bounced against something with a crack of glass.

Roland rolled to one side just as an ax blade bit into the ground where he'd been lying. He activated his rotary gun, spinning the barrels so fast they blurred, then twisted around and opened fire, spraying a circle of small-caliber shells around him.

The bullets careened off hidden Toth, disrupting their cloaks and exposing more than a dozen of the massive warriors.

"That's what they were shooting at," Roland said.

The Toth turned to face Roland, hissing and jabbing at him with their halberds as they spread out to surround him.

Roland returned the rotary gun to the shoulder housing and then pulled free the sword hilt locked to his thigh and activated the blade.

It was still unfolding when he leapt toward the largest Toth warrior.

"*Ferrum corde!*" Roland reversed the grip on the blade and

drove it into the Toth's face. He landed next to the warrior and dragged the body up to one side where it intercepted a halberd that cracked through the flank armor and embedded deep in the alien's flesh.

Roland ducked and ripped the blade out of the dead Toth, slicing it across another warrior's forelegs, severing them at the knees. He drove an uppercut into the wounded Toth and shattered its helm and skull in a spray of crystal.

A Toth brought its weapon up and angled the energy gun down toward Roland. The Templar swiped the flat of his blade through the air and knocked the weapon to one side as it fired. A bolt flashed past Roland and impacted another Toth in the chest.

Roland grabbed his blade and stepped toward the Toth, driving the tip into a seam in the crystal just above the neck. Yellow blood sprayed out against the inside of the armor and Roland twisted the sword free.

He fired his gauss cannons at a Toth charging at him, its weapon lowered like a lance. The rounds hit and the alien stumbled forwards.

Roland drove the tip of his sword into the ground and

seized the Toth with both hands. He lifted it off the ground and used its momentum to hurl the warrior into a pair of aliens with a satisfying crack of armor and bones.

He reached for his sword just as an axe blade struck his wrist. The blade passed through and his hand went limp as sparks shot out from the servos.

Roland planted a kick in his attacker's chest that launched it into a very quick flight against a tree. The Toth's spine snapped as it nearly wrapped around the trunk. With the crack of gauss cannons, Roland whirled around, grabbing the hilt with his other hand.

Nicodemus stood over the last of the Toth. He drove the tip of his sword into the throat of a warrior pinned beneath his boots.

"You missed linkup," the Templar said.

"I'll do better in the future." Roland twisted his hilt, snapping the blade back into the handle, and then joined Nicodemus as the older Armor ran toward the channel, boots crunching through fire-blackened bush and fallen branches.

They burst onto the beach where Martel and Morrigan stood back-to-back at the channel edge, firing at Toth as they closed toward them. Trinia was crouched between the Armor, her arms covering her head. Araki and Kataro emerged from farther down the beach.

"Toth are pushing on you," Murayama sent over the IR as target icons flooded onto Roland's HUD, like a red tide rolling toward their position from the east and west.

"Fire when ready," Martel sent.

"Principal says Cyrgal are still in the danger zone," Murayama said.

"They were warned." Martel fired over Roland's shoulder as he slid to a stop next to his lance commander, spraying Trinia with sand. Staying on one knee, Roland unfurled his shield from his left forearm housing. The Templar lance and half the Nisei formed a circle of iron around Trinia. Gauss cannons snapped as Toth warriors advanced through the hail of fire.

Plasma bolts from Cyrgal on the other island knocked Toth off their feet or exploded in a ball of steam against the ocean.

"They're not firing on us," Araki said.

"They need her alive," Martel said, "and they have bodies to spare."

Roland doubled-checked his HUD as his cannons reloaded.

The drones he and the other Armor had launched tracked thousands of Toth converging toward the channel.

"Shot in three…" Murayama sent.

Roland stomped a heel into the sand and his anchor spike telescoped down into the sand. An error message flashed across his HUD: the anchor hadn't found purchase.

"Got an issue here." Roland drew the spike back, shifted over a few feet, and tried again. Same result.

Nicodemus reached an arm under Roland's shoulder.

From their perch higher up the mountain, two Nisei fired their rail guns. The shells broke the sound barrier as they accelerated just beyond the ends of the twin firing vanes. Thunderclaps tore down the mountainside and the jungle swayed as if hit by a sudden hurricane.

The rail gun shells sliced through the sky, leaving a trail of burning air as they angled toward the ocean just beyond the wave line. The shells, designed to punch through capital-ship Armor, shot through the water and exploded against the ocean floor.

Roland watched as an enormous bubble of steam rose from the ocean and a tidal wave rolled toward him and the rest of the

Armor. The shock wave crushed Toth warriors, picking them up and adding them to the force of nature bearing down on Roland.

Toth on the shore looked back at the oncoming destruction. Most didn't even bother to try to outrun the inevitable.

Roland rammed his anchor heel into the sand again and felt the drill bit hit home, but a HUD icon flashed amber—only the tip had found purchase. The tidal wave grew closer, rising almost twenty feet as it reached the shallows just off the beach.

Roland braced his shield against his body just as the tidal wave hit. The impact felt like he'd stepped in front of a truck and his systems went mad with warnings. He felt the strain in his anchor and realized it wasn't going to hold.

The drill bit snapped apart and Roland bounced off Morrigan's shoulder as the water swept him away. The world rolled over and over and then went dark.

When he didn't feel like a leaf in the wind anymore, he lifted his helm up. Sand fell away from his optics.

The lower section of the island was a war zone of broken trees, scattered foliage and dead Toth warriors all around him. The ocean was flat, but frothy with sea foam.

"*Roland. Status report,*" Nicodemus asked through the IR.

"Recovering." Roland pushed himself up and his damaged wrist gave out. Rotating the rest of the servos, he heard the squeal of sand against the joints.

A Toth floundered in the sand, its tail kicking up dust until it righted itself. With much of its crystal armor ripped away by the wave, the Toth sniffed the air then dragged itself toward a lump in the sand.

Trinia sat up.

"The principal!" Roland brought his gauss cannons up and the ammo line flopped free from the housing on his back.

The Toth swiped at the Aeon…but the claws passed through her head and shoulder.

Cannons snapped and exit wounds burst from the alien's chest, spraying Trinia with yellow blood. Trinia's form flickered and shrank down to Marc Ibarra, his face covered with viscera.

"Nope!" Marc tried to wipe himself clean and struggled out of the wet sand. "Done! All done being your bait!"

Roland looked back to the Armor, all of whom were covered in a thin layer of wet sand.

"It worked." Martel lifted his anchor out of the surf and snapped the spike back into the housing. "Got the Toth to mass where we could hit them with the big guns. Why are you complaining?"

Marc nudged the eviscerated Toth with his foot, and it ripped at the sand in death throes.

"Nope!" Marc turned and ran back up the mountain to the village.

"Nicodemus, Roland," Martel said, "back to the Aeon and provide security. Rest of us will sweep the beach for Toth survivors."

Roland looked down at his broken anchor and withdrew it back into his leg. Nicodemus, who looked little worse for wear, helped him to his feet.

"Any regrets joining the Ibarra Nation?" Nicodemus asked as they trudged up the pathway.

"Wouldn't have it any other way," Roland said, limping slightly as sand worked its way out of his Armor.

Chapter 20

Rain spattered against the cobblestones as Nicodemus and Roland returned to the village. Distant thunder sounded weak compared to the clash of battle they'd just been through.

A pair of Nisei stood guard on either side of Trinia's hut, which had collapsed, blown aside by the pressure wave caused by the Nisei's rail guns. The Aeon sat next to the clay oven in the middle of what remained, unfazed by the rain.

"Murayama," Nicodemus said, motioning to Roland, "you're the highest-rated here in field repairs."

"Sir." The Nisei swapped places with Nicodemus and lifted Roland's damaged arm. Sensor wands snapped out of Murayama's Armor and poked around the partially severed wrist.

"You should have made your house from brick," Marc said

to Trinia as raindrops smacked against his silver shoulders, freezing a few moments later.

"I was at peace," she said, "before you came here. My own little part of the cosmos to call my own, to reflect on a life of failure...and one success that didn't matter in the end. Then *you* and your agents of chaos show up." Trinia kicked a wooden spear at Marc. It bounced off his leg and clattered over the cobblestones.

"No one is alone, my dear," Marc said. "The Aeon had a good thing going, but the Xaros were coming for you. You fought back...and lost. You lost but you weren't beaten. You're never beaten, unless you give up. Now the Toth are here for you. They're not going to stop either. They smell prey and they'll keep hunting."

"The Aeon will slip into history while the Toth are still a plague on the stars." She shook her head. "There is no justice, is there?"

"Not for lack of trying on our part." Marc turned away and saw Roland. He snapped his head back to Trinia.

"Now the Cyrgal are suffering because of me," she said. "I don't know how many were killed on the beach. They should have listened to me when I warned them to stay away. They're a decent culture when they work together, but most of the time they're stubborn and so very naive."

"Come with us," Marc said. "The Toth will figure out you're gone, and if they move on the Cyrgal, they'll regret it. You'll be safe."

"You have a reputation when it comes to promises." Trinia looked up at him, rain streaming down her face. "I had a talk with your Nisei while you were setting up your ambush. Now I know why you were off the galactic stage for so long."

"I don't know *what* they told you," Marc said, pointing a finger at Murayama. "But let me explain!"

Murayama ignored him as arc welders unfolded from his arm.

"Treason?" she asked.

"Light…treason." Marc raised his hands next to his face. "It's all sorted out now, *isn't it?*"

"Lady Ibarra has him on parole," Nicodemus said. "He carries the Lady's word. All his promises will be fulfilled by her, by the Templar and by our nation."

"Stacey…" Trinia looked back to the long house and the

entrance to the underground lab. "She's taken to her role with the procedurals so strongly. Not like the woman I knew."

"She was barely into adulthood when you met her," Marc said. "She's come a long way since then. And she…she could use your help."

"The Lady needs nothing but us by her side," Nicodemus said. "She is rightly guided."

"How about we just speak when we're spoken to, yeah?" Marc asked.

"Motion detected." Kataro raised his cannon arm and backed up to shield Trinia.

Murayama's tools snapped back into his arm and he went to form a perimeter around the Aeon.

Roland flexed his hand. The fingers bent stiffly and he couldn't rotate the wrist, but the field-expedient repairs were better than nothing. He switched on his IR optics and scanned the jungle as it swayed in the storm.

"Martel and the others are en route," Nicodemus said.

"You'd think the Toth would have learned by now," Murayama said. "We do not yield. We do not bend. We do not fail.

We are Armor."

A shadow in the infrared slunk between trees in the distance.

"Move her back to the lab?" Kataro asked.

"They'll be waiting for her in there," Roland said. "We've the advantage in the open. They won't fire if there's any risk it would harm her."

"Use her as a human shield?" Marc asked. "So gallant of our Black Knight."

"No one spoke to you," Nicodemus said.

"Hypocrisy and sarcasm are just a few of my many talents," Marc snapped.

Gauss fire carried up the path from the beach.

"Trinia, is there any place that's fortified?" Nicodemus asked.

A faint ululation sounded through the jungle.

"The other island." She got up, putting her back to Nicodemus', and peered around Murayama's shoulder. "There's a landing zone in the caldera and lifts that should still be operational from the base of the volcano."

"The Cyrgal going to be a problem?" Roland asked.

"I'll declare you all my...guardian angels. They have a concept close to that," she said.

"Honored," Marc said, bowing slightly.

"Not you. You I'll dub a cherub. Or a trickster demon," she said.

"Leprechaun," Roland said. "Morrigan will love that."

"You are off my Christmas list. Again. Buddy," Marc said.

Lightning broke overhead, illuminating Toth warriors on top of the carved rock. One thrust a halberd into the sky and a ululation rose from hundreds of Toth as the warriors scrambled down the rock and more emerged from the jungle.

"Keep the perimeter." Nicodemus grabbed his hilt from his hip and unsnapped the blade. "Open fire. *Ferrum Corde!*"

The Armor blared the war cry from their speakers and Roland activated his rotary weapon. It spun to life as the others let off a volley of gauss fire into the charging ranks. The heavy-caliber shells blew through two Toth before embedding in a third.

Roland picked off warriors maneuvering from cover to cover in the jungle. The temptation to charge forward and give them the blade was palpable, but the Toth were betting on the Armor fighting like scared, undisciplined troops.

He flipped his rotary cannon around and slaved it to Murayama's targeting systems. The two Armors' weapons blazed with shells, spraying across the Toth at head level, cracking the crystal armor over their faces but not penetrating. Blinded Toth slowed, tripping up the others behind them as the gauss cannons decimated the charge.

A blur rose up from the ground and Roland swung a punch out of reflex, striking a warrior in the shoulder, crushing an armor plate and wrecking the cloak field. He grabbed it by the chest and activated his shield, the graphenium edge cutting through the Toth's armor and slicing open its throat.

Roland shoved it away as a wave of Toth warriors materialized out of the jungle.

"Shift fire!" Roland deactivated the safeties on his gauss cannons and slammed his other hand on top of the weapon, the gauss cannon snapping like a string of fireworks as it went full auto. His HUD filled with warnings as the barrels went red-hot.

Gauss shells scythed through the Toth, blasting them apart

as the recoil inched Roland back with each bolt.

Steam billowed from the weapon as it froze up. Sparks and thin tendrils of electricity stabbed from the capacitors.

"Frag out!" He pulled the emergency-release lever on the cannon, hurled it at the oncoming energy, then thrust his shield over Trinia as the cannon exploded.

Shrapnel pinged off Roland's Armor as a blast wave shoved his shield back. Trinia was on the ground, arms over her head, but she looked unharmed.

A Toth wrapped claws around Roland's shield and yanked it back with a hiss. Roland released it off his arm and the Toth found itself holding it over its head, a look of surprise on its face.

Roland punted it between the forelegs, sending it flying back, then he drew his sword with his offhand and raised it overhead.

Lightning broke overhead, casting shadows across the ground. The Toth facing Roland hesitated. The rain lessened, slowing to a sprinkle, and moonlight shown across the distant sea.

"Come on, you cowards." Roland leveled the blade at the nearest warrior, standing knee-deep in Toth dead. "Is that all you've got?"

The Toth snarled and charged forward, leaping at Roland and impaling itself on Roland's sword up to the hilt. Grabbing Roland's sword arm, the Toth wrenched to one side. Its weight pulled Roland off-balance and another warrior behind hurled its halberd at the Armor.

The throw went wide, and the crystalline weapon spun end over end toward Trinia. Roland reached for the weapon, his fingers brushing the haft as it went by.

Marc jumped in front of Trinia and took the blade to the chest with a crack, the ax blade embedding in his silver body. He stood for a moment and touched a crystal spike pointed just beneath his nose. Then he sank to his knees.

Gauss fire snapped as the rest of the Armor from the beach came over the hill, shooting down the last of the Toth.

"Marc?" Trinia went to her old friend. His surface rippled but there was no sound as he shoved weakly at the weapon in his chest.

Roland pulled back, still watching the jungle for the next threat.

Marc knocked on the back of Roland's leg then tapped the halberd.

"He wants it out." Trinia reached for the haft but Roland pushed her away and into Nicodemus.

Roland grabbed the alien weapon just behind the axe blade and it crackled with electricity. His arm went numb as his pod shut off feedback from his suit. He pulled the blade out slowly and tossed it aside.

A deep gash ran from Marc's collarbone to his solar plexus. Beneath his shell, bits of crystal crumbled out of the wound and bounced off his knees. Marc picked the pieces up and pressed them back into his chest.

"What can we do for him?" Roland asked.

"I don't...I don't know," Trinia said, rubbing her bare arms. Her breath frosted and she looked puzzled before she looked back to the steam rising off the Toth bodies.

"So cold," she said, backing away from Marc.

Roland felt a chill in his fingers, and sensors on his Armor showed the temperature plummeting.

"Back, everyone back," Nicodemus said.

Ice grew from Marc's body, cracking and snapping as it covered him and the surrounding ground like a far-from-complete sculpture.

"That's new," Morrigan said as the rest of the Armor arrived. She cocked the smoking barrels of her gauss cannon up next to her shoulder. "You're not supposed to throw your gun at the enemy, boy-o."

"Good idea at the time." Roland looked to Trinia. "Are you injured?"

"Nothing worth mentioning." She reached for Marc's icy enclosure but pulled her hand back with a look of pain on her face. "I knew how to load a mind into the matrix inside the bodies. The Qa'Resh never told me how they work beyond that."

"We can carry him back to Navarre." Colonel Martel looked to the sky, now almost cloudless and full of stars. "*Warsaw* has evac on the way."

"Monsters." The word came from a dozen different places behind them. Roland whirled around, his sword braced before him.

On the dead Toth littering the ground, an alien face appeared on the crystal armor. Not Toth.

The elegant, wide-eyed face of an Ixio.

"Humans bring pain and death wherever they go in the galaxy, Mistress Trinia," the Ixio said.

"I know that voice," Roland said. "Tomenakai. I thought I killed him on Oricon."

"You did," the alien responded. "But through Lord Bale I was Risen, and those who are Risen will forever serve the Kesaht. We have such wonders to share with you, Mistress Trinia. Do not side with these devils. Murderers. Those that nearly wiped out another race simply to save themselves. They are no better than the Xaros. Surely you see that."

"What's he talking about?" Trinia asked.

"A crime," Tomenakai said, "one that must be atoned with the end of humans. Lord Bale will explain it to you in person. Leave the metal abominations and join the Kesaht."

"You think I don't know what the Toth have done? What they do to those they capture? Never," she said.

"Lies. All human lies to justify their crimes," the Ixio said. "You are more valuable to the Kesaht than you know. But if you need some encouragement, look to the first moon."

The Cyrgal inhabited moon hung a few handbreadths over the horizon, half in darkness, the surface settlements shining brightly on the surface. A point grew even brighter and Trinia gasped. The city flashed and went dark.

"Fusion warhead," Nicodemus said.

"Stop!" Trinia shouted. "Stop! They're no threat to you."

"Eighty-five million Cyrgal—correction, eighty million Cyrgal—live on that moon," Tomenakai said. "How low must that number go before you cooperate?"

Another blast flashed over the moon's horizon.

"No!" Trinia reached toward the moon and then stopped, bringing her hands down next to her thighs. She stooped forward slightly.

"I...am eleven thousand years old," she said. "I watched as billion after countless billion were lost to the Xaros. I lived with the despair of my own people dying right in front of me. You think...you think *this* can move me?"

"All will serve the Kesaht," Tomenakai said. "Lord Bale would incorporate the Cyrgal as best they can offer...or they will be exterminated as vermin. Our ascension is inevitable."

"Evac transport arrives in five minutes," Martel sent over the IR to keep the message from the Ixio.

"See what you have wrought," the Ixio said and the image on the crystal armor switched to a Cyrgal broadcast of fires and chaos in a city beneath the moon's surface. Trinia turned away.

The ice around Marc cracked and fell away like a frozen cocoon. The silver man crawled out and rolled onto the ground. The gash in his chest was gone.

"That," Marc said, "was not pleasant. At all."

"You're good to move?" Roland asked.

"Never better." Marc ran a hand over where the wound had been.

"Beach," Martel sent. *"Can't get a Destrier in here. Move out."*

****

Armor formed a perimeter around Trinia and Marc, and every time another nuke exploded, Roland glanced up at the moon. Just how many Cyrgal had been killed…he didn't want to know.

A Destrier transport crested the horizon, flying low enough

over the ocean that it kicked up a wake of sea spray.

"Recovery on the move," Martel said. "Evac can't spare the power for a full stop. Step lively."

"What does that mean?" Trinia asked.

"Ramp comes down," Marc said, rolling his shoulders back and forth, "transport slows just enough for us to run on board as it passes."

"That…no…I'm not that fast," she said.

"I'll carry you," Morrigan said to her. "Roland. You've got him."

"Can someone else, maybe possessing a bit of grace, please take—"

Morrigan shot a hand toward Marc, thumb and fingers spaced just wide enough to grip his head, and pinched her fingertips together.

"Hint taken," Marc said.

"I remember the Toth," Trinia said, "when they tried to capture a Qa'Resh. They were going to murder it, satisfy their addiction for neural energy. They were Bastion's greatest mistake…and the galaxy still suffers for it."

A keening wail carried down the beach as Cyrgal ran onto the sand, tearing at their clothes and waving to the moon. More picked their way through the wrecked jungle and called out to Trinia.

"Please don't." She stepped behind Martel. "I can't stand to see them suffering like this. They share pain in a way humans and Aeon can't understand."

Cyrgal stopped on the other end of the channel, in near hysterics as they pleaded to Trinia. None stepped into the water.

Old memories dredged up through Roland's mind, families grieving for all those lost on Earth, his own personal emotions for his lost parents—first his father dying in deep space, then his mother perishing on Luna during the second Xaros invasion. Neither's body was ever recovered. Such a thing was common during the Ember War, but a dark, vulnerable place in him wished to lament at a parent's side to make letting go that much easier.

His animosity toward the Cyrgal faded away, but he still watched for any sign of hostility.

"Pickup in sixty seconds," Martel said.

A patch of blue light appeared on the ocean just ahead of

the transport.

"Pull up!" Nicodemus shouted. "Tell them to—"

A Toth plasma bolt erupted out of the water and blew through the cockpit. The ship lurched down and crashed into the ocean, tearing apart as it flipped over and over like a stone skipping across a pond. The fuselage sank a few hundred yards away, buttressed by crashing waves.

A Toth ship, larger than a Mule and bristling with diamond-shaped cannons, emerged from the sea. Water sloughed off the top and came down in curtains around it.

Cyrgal opened fire with their plasma rifles, singeing black streaks across the hull and accomplishing little else. A hatch on the bottom of the ship opened and a quad-barreled weapon swung out and opened fire, peppering the Cyrgal on the beach and sending them off in a rout.

Morrigan stomped an anchor into the ground and brought her rail gun up and over her shoulder.

"Fire that here, it'll kill her," Nicodemus said.

"Seem to be out of options," Morrigan said.

Trinia ran from the Armor and went to a Toth body half-buried in the sand. She brushed a segment of the cracked crystal clear and slapped a palm against it.

"Tomenekai, do you hear me? I surrender, you understand? I surrender!" she shouted.

The Ixio's face appeared on the armor, cracked to match the damaged surface.

"No, Trinia! You can't!" Marc darted around Araki's grasp.

"Wait…" Roland stepped toward the pair when his Armor froze. His HUD dissolved and the world faded into a white abyss, like he was going through a Crucible wormhole.

+Let her go.+

He'd felt this once before—what felt like a lifetime ago—during a battle with the Vishrakath.

Saint Kallen.

The beach returned and Roland stumbled forward, his every nerve humming. He looked over to the rest of the Armor; all were just as stunned as he was.

"Let her go," Martel said. "Let her go, Marc!" The colonel stomped forward and grasped the metal man by the shoulder and hauled him back.

"I'll go with you," Trinia said to the Kesaht. "But you must let them live. Let the rest of the Cyrgal live. You understand?"

Tomenakai turned his head from side to side, focusing his oversized eyes on her one at a time.

"Agreed," he said.

"You see this?" She touched her brooch. "Poison. You break our deal, I'll be dead before I hit the ground. Then you'll have nothing but a war with the Cyrgal for all your trouble. See how Bale rewards you then."

"An Ixio keeps his word," Tomenakai said and the crystal screen fizzled away.

"Are you all insane?" Marc asked. "She can't—"

Martel squeezed his shoulder.

Trinia, her pallor light, almost ashen now, darted her gaze from Marc to the approaching Toth ship. She put one hand in the sand and then brushed them clean.

"I'm sorry, Marc," she said. "I did wish to see Stacey again. Remember me well. Remember the Aeon well."

She ran into the ocean and was up to her knees in surf when the Toth ship hovered overhead. A ramp lowered and a Toth warrior hauled her up and into the ship. He dragged her away, Marc's cries lost in the engine noise.

Morrigan kept her rail gun trained on the ship as it rose into the air.

"Don't," Martel said.

"I'd never. I heard Her," Morrigan said. "Just for appearances."

"We all heard her?" Roland asked.

The silence from the Armor was all the answer he needed.

"'Heard'?" Marc kicked Martel in the shin. "What is wrong with all of you?"

"Saint Kallen," Nicodemus said. "She…commanded us."

"She did?" Marc stopped, dumbfounded, then shrugged the shoulder in Martel's grasp and was released. He went over to the dead Toth where Trinia had spoken to the Ixio and pawed through the sand, picking up Trinia's necklace and giving it a quick shake.

"Why leave that behind?" Roland asked.

"Because it's what we needed," Marc said. "I started off as an inventor. A scientist. And I don't care what species you are—a true master of knowledge keeps notes. These are data crystals.

Thousands of years of work with Qa'Resh technology all right here."

"The Toth still have her," Roland said. "What do we do now?"

"Saint Kallen's got us this far," Marc said. "Keep the faith, son…and pray for Trinia."

Chapter 21

While the Dragoons were stopped in a wadi—a dried-out riverbed—at the base of a mountain, Santos scraped black soil out of the grooves of his anchor bit. The storms had passed, and the sky was full of the great swath of the Milky Way. Umbra was closer to the galactic center than Earth, and he'd never seen a night sky like the one above.

Aignar sat with his back to the dirt wall, his gauss cannons between his feet as he repaired the chamber mechanism. Gideon was at the end of the wade, his head and shoulder in defilade against the side.

"It always like this?" Santos asked as his anchor snapped back into his heel.

"What exactly?" Aignar asked without looking up.

"Confusion. Killing. Never-ending pressure." Santos ran a diagnostic on his weapon systems and grew concerned at his low ammo reserves.

"I've had it better and I've had it worse," Aignar said. "Your old man saw the elephant. He never spoke to you about it?"

"No. He never even let me watch his first movie, that *Last Stand on Takeni*. Which is odd, as Mr. Standish let customers at his liquor store download his recut version of the film. Dad was a lot prouder of all those romantic comedy movies he made later. He didn't even want to do commentary on the twentieth anniversary edition, but Standish threatened to cut off his under-the-table payments if he didn't."

"That movie is a propaganda piece," Aignar said. "Barely has Armor in it. They could've added more of the Smoking Snakes, but—wait…under-the-table payments?"

"Thirty-some child-support payments," Santos said. "Mr. Standish is a good guy…he knew all of us were being taken care of, but he also didn't want his spokesman living in some studio apartment in some Tucson shithole. Bad for the image."

"I never met Standish," Aignar said. "Now, Roland said

he…never mind."

"Roland the Black Knight?" Santos asked. "The one that defected to the Ibarras?"

"The traitor." Aignar leveled a finger, then rubbed the jawline on his helm. "He's gone. You're here now. Don't bring him up again." He slapped the gauss cannon assembly onto his forearm and connected the ammo line running into the magazines beneath his back.

"Sorry," Santos said.

"Drop incoming," Gideon said.

Santos's HUD pinged as traces of orbital drops appeared. He got up, hearing his servos grind with dirt, projecting the landing zones.

"We're nowhere near any of these," he said. "How many other lances are out here?"

"Just us," Gideon said. "But a few dozen extra pods, landing over an extended area…"

"Is a bluff that we're not alone," Aignar said, "and it gives them too many options for our true resupply point. If they try and investigate them all, they'll spread themselves thin looking for us.

One pod landing on top of us is a nice big kick-me sign."

"Now the hard part," Gideon said. "The Risen could have made it to one of two bolt holes."

A map came up in Santos's HUD, and he saw two spots pinged along a highway leading to the wrecked spaceport.

"The northernmost location was larger and closer to where we ambushed the column," Gideon said. "Orbitals saw mechanized infantry moving in before the storms hit. Southern bolt hole was smaller, but tanks and artillery were detected in there."

"Which would the Risen go to?" Aignar said.

"He ran off with his tail between his legs when we showed up," Santos said. "If he thought we were on his heels, you think he'd want Rakka to protect him?"

"Decent observation," Gideon said.

"Why even move?" Aignar asked. "Risen must have heard the supply depot was slagged. He burns fuel moving armor off the front lines and he risks getting caught out when the sun comes up…in a few Earth days. Shelter in place. Wait for logistics to come back on line."

"Never wait for the enemy to act," Gideon said. "Force

them into making a bad decision. That's why General Kendall ordered an offensive down this movement corridor."

A blue arrow stabbed out from Union lines down toward the Risen's valley.

"Kesaht don't have the bullets or fuel for an extended fight," Gideon said. "They either die in place or they retreat."

"Both," Aignar said. "Sanheel don't give a damn if Rakka die. Risen are the highest echelon in their society. They'll leave the infantry at the north end of the valley to hold off our attack, giving them time to escape south."

"Agreed," Gideon said. Map tiles flashed as the captain sorted through the terrain.

"What about an air evacuation?" Santos asked. "Send a shuttle out to get the VIP out of danger."

"You don't know Sanheel," Aignar said. "Prideful. Arrogant. It's one thing to 'advance in the other direction' out of a battle when it's obvious they'll lose. But waving to your troops as you skip town is admitting defeat. Hurts their standing within the hierarchy. When you're functionally immortal, your reputation's the only thing you've really got."

"MacArthur got a Medal of Honor for the failed defense of the Philippines," Santos said. "He never forgave the general that surrendered to the Japanese. Funny how all that works."

"And Napoleon snuck back to France to control the narrative before word of his loss in Egypt could catch up," Gideon said. "It's normally a mistake to overlay our culture onto aliens, but hierarchies exist across nature. Kesaht are no exception. If this was an Ixio Risen, our plan would change."

"Bunch of cowards," Aignar said.

"Then where do we—" A screech in the air interrupted Santos. A drop pod came down on the other side of a hill and struck with a *whoomph*.

"Resupply," Gideon said as he waved an arm forward and ran over the hill.

The pod was a rough-cut sphere with twenty sides with a diameter slightly taller than their suits. Metal pinged and smoked in the slight crater it generated on landing. Gideon ran a hand along a pod face and a small panel popped open. Data lines snaked out of his wrist and into ports.

"Gather round," Gideon said. "Self-destruct countdown

paused, but we can't tarry."

"How long's the timer?" Santos backed up to the pod and the flat sides fell open. Servo arms extended from inside and began repairing the dents and hole in his Armor.

"Eight minutes," Gideon said. "Then this crater gets a lot bigger."

Fresh ammo magazines went into his weapon housings, and Santos's mood perked up as the round counters rose and went green. His amniosis swirled as fresh fluid injected into his pod.

"These things figure out some way to rub my shoulders, I'll marry it," Aignar said.

His lance mates turned their helms to him.

"Don't judge me," Aignar said.

"Intel dump came with the pod," Gideon said. "Damn it…intelligence put a 'low probability' that the Risen moved during the storm and made it to the Kesaht base in IV Corps' sector. Air assets are being redirected there."

"Those weenies have no idea what it's like out here," Aignar said. "They think they know a storm when they've been in the same bunker sucking down coffee and hot food since they got on world?"

"What does that mean for us, sir?" Santos asked.

"Kesaht fighters," Gideon said. "If we pick up an air threat, cavalry's not coming anytime quick...and the attack that's going to run smack into the Rakka infantry will be hurting for air support."

"They'll figure it out when all the Kesaht fighters are over this valley protecting the Risen, right?" Santos asked.

"Time slows down when you're waiting for air support," Aignar said. "Doesn't seem to for the enemy."

"There's a forest on the Risen's route of march," Gideon said, sending a waypoint to their HUDs. "We'll have some top cover there."

"Well," Aignar said, raising his gauss cannon arm and stepping away from the drop pod, "when we're up to our eyeballs in crescent fighters, we'll know we've found the Risen."

"Let's move," Gideon said.

****

Being buried alive was oddly comforting for Santos. His suit lay face down in a shallow depression, his back covered by dirt and loose branches thrown on by Aignar before the other Iron Dragoon moved off to his own position elsewhere in the small forest.

He'd gone through the Long Dark of the sensory-deprivation pods during training, days on end of nothing but the abyss and his own thoughts. The training was meant to steel him against his suit being disabled and left on the battlefield until rescue and recovery…whenever that might happen.

A story had circulated while he was a trainee at Knox about a pod recovered by a Pathfinder on some ice ball during one of the skirmishes with the Naroosha. The lone Pathfinder—the rest of his team killed in action—dragged a pod for almost twenty-five miles through hostile territory, not knowing if the soldier inside was alive or dead.

None of the cadre ever confirmed or denied the tale, and the cadets had speculated whether the ambiguity was meant to heighten anxiety during the Long Dark (they all faced the same question: just how long could they wait before going insane or asphyxiating in their pod when the amniosis ran out of oxygen) or if the rumors of the story's connection to the Templar and Saint Kallen had something to do with it.

With his suit powered down and his only external feed coming from a small optic periscope and his IR connection to his lance, Santos was as well-hidden as a fifteen-foot metal killing machine could be in the forest. No need to move or breathe. He could remain in this position for weeks on end…though he was certain they'd find the Risen before that.

The forest hugged one side of the valley, clinging to a deep stream running down from the mountain. The next ridge over was a few miles away, its terrain consisting of windswept rocks offering little in the way of cover but shallow dips.

"New guy," Aignar sent over the IR, "whatever you do, don't think about all the worms in the soil. I saw them when I was covering you. They're huge. Like damn pythons. Sharp pointy teeth and slimy...so slimy."

"I know I'm the new guy," Santos said, "and I know when you're just messing with me."

"I'm *serious*," Aignar said.

Santos was certain he heard a giggle.

"Watch your sector," Gideon sent. The lance commander was farther back in the forest, well away from their vantage points.

A seismic sensor in his suit registered a detection.

"Got something," Santos said. "Low and steady. Consistent with Kesaht tanks."

"Dust on the horizon," Gideon said. "Column on approach."

Santos nibbled on his lower lip, an old trick he'd used to keep his mind alive in the sensory-deprivation tanks that developed into a nervous habit. They'd had the drop on the first Kesaht force they ambushed: Nova shells, close quarters—a fight Armor was designed to dominate and win.

Fighting on open terrain against Kesaht tanks was not how his lance would survive. Gideon wanted a precision strike on the Risen and then a quick exit up the valley…but if the Kesaht detected them somehow, the scales would quickly fall out of their favor.

"Company plus of heavy tanks." Aignar sent images of the lead elements of the Kesaht column: over a dozen of the double-turreted vehicles, moving at a decent speed for something so massive. Another image of Sanheel warriors—hundreds at a gallop just behind the tanks—followed.

"Good thing we ammo'd up," Aignar said. "Might not have had enough bullets for them all. Tanks are slowing…Sanheel coming around the flank and heading for the forest. Scouting force is my guess."

"Maintain cover," Gideon said. "We need to identify and kill the Risen. We're in a better position if we kill him with our first shot."

"Thinking quiet thoughts," Aignar said. "If you hear Sanheel getting murdered, you know they found me."

"Orders understood," Santos said. The quality of his hasty camouflage suddenly became very important to him. Armor weren't subtle in their employment or actions. Hiding in the bushes was for Pathfinders.

The lead tanks came into view, travelling in groups of five arrayed in a wedge formation. Santos zoomed in on the dust-caked vehicles, looking for anything distinctive that would mark out the Risen's vehicle.

"Should be three times as many tanks," Aignar said, "based

on what was spotted during our crunchies' last fight."

"As if this tactical problem wasn't enough? You want more tanks?" Santos asked.

"Fuel," Gideon said. "They're moving as fast as they can work the engines. Inefficient. Burns more fuel than a slower pace. Risen chose speed over more tanks to escort him."

"Scouts entering the forest," Aignar said.

Santos held his optic line steady. It was thin as a straw and a subdued gray, and he had worked it through a bush with tiny needles for concealment. He wasn't certain how sharp Sanheel eyesight was, but a human would have to practically trip on it before they realized something was amiss in the foliage.

His instructors' reminders about assumptions being the root cause of all failures played in the back of his mind. He considered withdrawing the scope, but then he would be deaf and blind while buried in a shallow grave. The lance needed him to find the Risen, not cower in a hole.

The clomp of hooves rumbled through the forest as a pair of Sanheel brushed past his location, both carrying long rifles with bayonets beneath an arm. He felt a slight vibration through his pod as another pair slowed to a stop near him.

An alien wandered right in front of his optic line. The Sanheel was large, a little over nine feet tall, with a single tusk protruding from the left side of its dust-caked face. When it snorted and shook its head like a wet dog, dust flew off and formed a brief cloud around its shoulders. It wiped the back of a hand across a meaty face and rested its flank against a tree trunk. Loose strands of thick hair partially covered the skull implant over one ear. Wires connected an earpiece to equipment built into the shoulder armor.

"Kal ora min darra," it rumbled and set the butt of its rifle against the ground.

Santos activated his suit's translation software. The Terran Union had picked up enough Sanheel and Ixio transmissions to piece together their language, something they hadn't managed with the Rakka yet.

"We rest and we invite the storm," another Sanheel said from off to one side. Santos didn't move the optic line for fear the movement might catch their eyes.

"This isn't home," the first said, drawing a line off a

shoulder and putting it in its mouth. It spat out muddy water and then took a long draught. "All of us made the run across the Plain of Blood for the trials. Done in a single sun's pass. This ball of manure is nothing but a pain in my hooves in all directions, save for ugly mountains. We can run until we drop dead before this place's suns rise again."

"And if we haven't delivered Risen Nargas to his peers by suns' rise, we will die," the other Sanheel said as it came into view. He bore a sash over one shoulder, adorned with carvings of metal and bone. "Fail like that and our Risen will not remember us to the great Unity."

The target's here, at least, Santos thought.

The first raised a forehoof and plucked a flint of rock out from the ornate shoe nailed into it.

"You'd rather have made this journey in your tank, yes?" the second asked.

"It is better to fight on your legs than in a box filled with your crew's passed gas," the first said. "That Risen Nargas chose to join the horde instead of take his own tank…"

Santos stiffened inside his pod. The target wasn't within the protection of a tank?

"He cares enough to share the difficulty of a long run with us," the second said, "those that had to leave their tanks behind. We are lucky to have him. An Ixio would have us carry him on our backs, like a beast of burden."

"It is the demons," the first said as he put the water line back on his shoulder. "They nearly sent his soul back to Lord Bale when he was in his tank. They will strike those first. That is why he runs beside us."

"Can it not be both?" The second punched the other in the shoulder.

"It can."

Santos tapped out a text message for his lance but didn't send it. Sending a transmission, even a tight-beam IR, with the Sanheel so close risked detection.

Kesaht tanks rumbled past the forest, leaving a trail of dust in their wake.

"I can't believe the demons wrecked the supply yard," a Sanheel said as he removed a small rectangle wrapped in foil from its belt. "Nothing but freeze-dried Rakka jerky to eat."

"Our thralls are good for something," the other said. "Especially if you get the spicier packets from home."

Santos wasn't sure if "Rakka jerky" meant jerky made from Rakka or made by Rakka. He let that question slide as an error in the translation software.

The Sanheel with the sash touched its earpiece.

"Torsh found footprints farther back," it said. "Too large for the murderers' skull soldiers or scouts. Demons."

"Torsh is a whelp that sees demons everywhere," the first said. "It could be feral cyber Rakka or some local wildlife. Don't bother the Risen until someone with *ugirish* on their *dandan* can confirm." It opened the foil packet and took a bite from the densely packed black jerky inside.

A crack sounded across the valley and one of the tanks lurched to a halt.

"What was that?" The Sanheel dropped its food and hefted its rifle to a shoulder.

"Came from across the valley," the other said.

Smoke poured out of the seams in the stopped tank's turret just before it exploded, sending the tubes spinning through the air.

Another crack sounded through the echoes of the explosion and another tank burst into flames.

Santos tried to make sense of the attack. There was no way Gideon was the one firing with what sounded like a Mauser heavy rifle.

"Demons!" The Sanheel with the sash touched its earpiece. "Fire coming from the other side of the valley. The Risen is coming here to-to direct the battle."

The Kesaht tanks swung toward the firing, exposing their weaker back armor to the forest.

"Warn the Risen," the first said, "in case the whelp is right about the enemy being in these woods."

The Sanheel with the sash hesitated.

Santos sent off a burst text transmission and swept his arm back through the soil to the hilt locked to his thigh.

"What was that?" The second Sanheel peered over the bush toward the ground disturbance and looked right at the lens of Santos's optic.

Santos snapped the device back into his helm and burst out of the ground. He stabbed the sashed Sanheel with his gladius, pinning it through the chest to a tree. Yanking the blade free, Santos spun around on his waist servos, decapitating the other with a single stroke.

Both Sanheel collapsed to the ground.

"Gideon, Aignar, did you monitor my last?" he asked over the IR.

Booms from the Kesaht tanks sounded through the forest.

"About to have company," Aignar said. "Every last Sanheel on foot is coming right for me."

"Moving!"

"—fire! Falling ba—" Gideon's garbled transmission came over the IR.

Santos ran through the forest toward Aignar's position. Pistons drove his legs hard, but dodging trees slowed him down. The report of Sanheel rifles and gauss cannons carried past him.

"Aignar? What's your status?" Santos asked as he shoulder-bumped off a tree and burst through a thick hedgerow.

The solid ground he'd anticipated on the other side of the bush was missing, and he fell forward into a deep embankment cut out by the stream feeding the forest.

He landed with a splash in water that came halfway up to his knees. The five Sanheel running along the other bank looked just as surprised as Santos felt.

Santos's feet sank into the mud, but he kept his momentum moving forward, albeit slowly. His gauss cannons hit a Sanheel in the flank, punching it against the other embankment.

A Sanheel, wearing a sash adorned with more carvings than the last one he saw, snarled and charged into the stream, clutching his bayonet-equipped rifle beneath an arm like a lance. Two of the Sanheel followed him, their hooves splashing through the water.

The last remained on the bank and fired. A round hit the front of Santos's helm and sent a wash of static across his HUD.

Disoriented, Santos fired a single gauss round into the stream and blew out a geyser. He drew his hilt and twisted the pommel to reform the blade into a longsword.

The high-ranking Sanheel burst through the water and stabbed its bayonet into the Armor's breastplate. Santos twisted to one side and the blade scraped across his chest. The alien had redirected the blow at the last second and landed only a glancing hit.

Santos swung his longsword up and hit the bottom of the rifle with the flat of his blade, sending the Sanheel's weapon flying. The higher-ranked warrior kept moving forward until it was just past the armor. It dug its forward hooves into the streambed and its back legs kicked out, striking Santos in the chest. The force of the blows launched him backwards and he landed with a splash.

Water washed over his optics.

He rolled to one side out of reflex and another Sanheel's forward hooves crashed into the water where he'd been a moment ago. He gripped a handful of mud as he kept rolling and tossed it into the face of the Sanheel that almost killed him. The black goo hit with a wet smack as a rifle shot bounced off Santos's shoulder with a spark.

The Armor got up to a crouch, mud and water sloughing off his back and helmet, and he growled through his speakers.

Snapping to one side, he caught the foreleg of a Sanheel just before it could strike. A twist of his torso ripped the alien's leg off and it fell into the stream with a screech. He flung the severed limb at the shooter on the bank, knocking the rifle to one side.

A single gauss shot hit the shooter in the shoulder and blood splattered against the embankment. The shell passed through its body and buried deep in the soil with a thump. The muddy foe cleared its vision just in time to look down the cannon's other barrel and see the capacitor flash just before its head was blown off.

"Demon!" The ranked Sanheel had recovered its rifle and was charging across the stream, bayonet leveled.

Santos brought his sword to one hip, the blade angled behind his body. He dropped to a fighting stance and held his ground. The Armor timed the Sanheel's charge and swung his sword up with a speed his flesh and blood could never have matched.

The strike cut through the Sanheel's rifle then slashed it from hip to shoulder. Blood arced off Santos's sword tip as the alien stumbled past. The forward half of the rifle splashed in the stream as the alien's sash fell loose and floated away with the current.

The Sanheel toppled over. Dead. Blood stretched into a long ribbon through the water.

"Kid!" Aignar called out from the embankment. Smoke rose

from his cannon barrels and his weapon was configured into a spiked mace, splattered with blood. "I was worried about you."

"I thought you were on the forest perimeter. You get my alert?"

"Yeah. You get my mine?"

An image of Kesaht crescent fighters in a distant sky snapped up on Santos's HUD.

"Bogies inbound," Aignar said, pointing into the woods, "which is why I pulled back. We need to draw them in deeper. Use the forest for cover until we can find the Risen. If he hunkers down in the open with fighters protecting him…tough nut to crack."

He ran up the stream bank and Santos followed.

"Who the hell is out there picking off tanks?" he asked. "Where'd Gideon go? I know he didn't leave us behind."

"The captain knows what he's—"

The thunder crack of a rail gun sent a weak blast wave through the forest, disturbing branches overhead.

Santos looked toward where the shot came from. "That's from the other side of the valley," he said.

"Now I get it," Aignar said. "That's the hammer." He beat against his chest. "We're the anvil."

The snap of branches and a rustle of brush came from the north. Sanheel, dozens of them, worked their way through the forest.

A pair of enemy fighters tore overhead, so low they almost scraped the treetops. They pulled up into a vertical climb, disappearing into the night sky.

Aignar pulled Santos over the embankment and they took cover from the Sanheel behind trees.

"Think the fighters saw us?" Santos asked.

"Better assume they did than get strafed later," Aignar said. "Still might get strafed. But somehow, it'll be better if it isn't a surprise."

"Stand by for rail shot!" Gideon said over the IR. *"I need close air defense immediately following while I recharge for the next round."*

"He's doing *what?*" Santos asked through his speakers. "A second shot while anchored? He'll be a sitting duck!"

"Which is why he wants air defense. From us. In the middle of the forest." Aignar looked up at the thick branches. He put a hand against a trunk and his mace snapped into an axe.

"You know how many trees we'd have to knock down to get a clear shot of the whole sky?" Santos asked.

"Sturdy. Deep roots. Should hold me." Aignar looked at Santos. "I'm going to need your mortar case."

"Are you out of your mind?" Santos peeked around the trunk to the Sanheel milling around in the distance.

"Keep them off me," Aignar said and then switched to the lance IR channel. "Gideon, roger on air defense. Give me ninety seconds before shot."

"Sixty," Gideon sent back.

"Knew he'd say that. Kid, get on the other side and push. Aim for the monster of a tree behind me." Aignar hit his axe against the trunk with a crack, embedding the blade deep into the wood. He pried it out and hit again, cutting out a wedge.

"If I don't know what's happening, no way the enemy does either," Santos muttered, rushing around the tree as Aignar hit it again. The Sanheel hadn't noticed yet, a boon the Armor attributed to the echo of tank fire coming from the valley. He put his hands against the trunk and shoved, bringing every hydraulic and servo in his suit to bear.

The tree cracked and groaned as it fell.

"Left! Left!" Aignar shouted.

Santos dug his fingers into the bark and guided it to the left. The tree crashed into the upper branches of a taller one and came to a rest, angled up into the sky.

"Mortars!" Aignar whacked the back of Santos's Armor. He popped the ammunition cover and Aignar pulled the inner case out, slapping it onto his back, where it mag-locked into place. He climbed up the partially fallen tree and got to the top. Leaves and sticks rained down on Santos as Aignar cleared branches away with his axe.

"What the hell are you doing?" Santos asked. Shouts were coming from the distant Sanheel.

"Mortars come with variable fuses. Point detonating. Radar range finders for air burst. You know you can set them manually too?" Aignar asked.

"I think that was during next week's gunnery training," Santos said.

"I'm going to use our mortars as field-expedient air defense.

Don't worry about—son of a bitch—there's one!"

The rumble of jet engines grew and red-hot bullets snapped over Aignar's head. He activated the shield in his forearm housing and rounds bounced off it. His rotary gun snapped onto his shoulder and opened fire. There was a boom and a Kesaht crescent fighter flew overhead, trailing black smoke and rolling over and over. It tore through treetops and exploded a hundred yards away.

Aignar lifted a foot and his anchor spike embedded into the trunk. His helm snapped toward the nearby mountain.

"Kid, hold on to—"

A blast wave from Gideon's rail shot swept through the forest and slapped Santos against Aignar's perch. The trunk started rolling over.

"Kid! Kid!"

Santos wrapped both arms around the trunk and heaved back, righting Aignar on the top, his servos straining to keep a grip.

"That's great, hold it steady," Aignar said.

A cloud of atomized rock rose up from the valley.

"What's happening out there?" Santos asked.

"I'm realizing this idea was a lot better in my head," Aignar said, crouching on the trunk and gripping it. He pointed his suit's internal mortar tube toward the valley. "But an OK plan, violently executed, is better than the perfect solution five minutes too late. There we go…fighters massing for an attack run on Gideon."

A rifle round snapped through the air and blew splinters off the tree just above Santos's grip.

"Enemy inbound," he called out.

"Hold them off!" A mortar spat out of Aignar's tube with a *bloomp* and more rounds fired in quick succession.

Santos aimed his gauss cannons in the general direction of the Sanheel attack and fired two rounds. The trunk listed to one side before he got control of it again.

"Hey!" Aignar shouted as an empty mortar case landed next to Santos.

"You want me to hold you steady or hold them off?"

"Both!"

The crump of exploding mortars echoed through the forest, mingling with rifle shots from the Sanheel and the residual roar of the rail gun still sounding off the mountains.

A bullet whacked against the top knuckle of his right middle finger, twisting the digit into an ugly angle as more shots snapped past his helm. He shrank back behind the trunk and looked to one side: nothing. To the left: glimpses of Sanheel galloping through the forest in the distance.

"We're getting flanked," Santos said. "Anytime you want to—"

A round punched into his side, ringing his internal pod like a bell.

"Fire solution loaded…don't move!" Aignar shouted.

A dozen Sanheel tore through the forest, rifles lowered like lances as a war cry rose from their throats. Fire from the other group cut off.

The tree rumbled as Aignar's mortar sent shells into the air. They exploded directly overhead with small puffs of black smoke, sending shrapnel through the air and into Kesaht fighters coming in low over the treetops.

A hunk of a mortar shell thumped into Santos's shoulder, embedding in the suit and smoking.

"Done?" Santos released the tree and went to one knee, swinging his Mauser off his back. He fired from the hip and struck a smaller tree, shattering the trunk into a thousand splinters that sprayed the charging Sanheel.

Another blast of overpressure from a rail gunshot slapped him from behind, pushing his Mauser barrel into the dirt.

"Fuuuu—" Aignar's tree rolled over, pushed by the blast. Santos reached up with his free hand but missed it by inches. The tree broke through the supporting branches and fell with a groan.

Aignar fell from the sky and landed in a cloud of dust. The tree crashed to the ground a few yards ahead of Aignar, sending up a brown fog.

"I'm good," Aignar said. "Sort of."

Santos felt the rumble of hooves through the ground. Sanheel shouted warnings and he heard bodies smack into the fallen tree. He fired his Mauser at shoulder level and racked another round.

The dust cleared, and he saw that the Sanheel charge had come to a stop at the sudden palisade. Santos shot another high-caliber round into the chest of an alien mashed against the trunk. The round passed through its back and punched through the alien behind it.

Aignar snapped to his feet and chopped his axe over the trunk and into the shoulder of an enemy, embedding it in flesh. He dragged the Sanheel over and tossed it aside with a flick of his wrist.

"For Novis!" Santos fired his Mauser again, exploding a Sanheel's head, and charged forward. He vaulted over the trunk, kicking an enemy in the jaw hard enough to snap its neck. He put two gauss cannon rounds point-blank into another chest as he landed and kicked the dying foe into two of its fellows.

Sanheel at the back of the scrum turned and ran as Aignar's Mauser blasted through an alien's flank.

Santos's vision went red as he tossed his heavy rifle up and caught it by the barrel. He swung it like a club at an alien that tried to block the strike by bracing its rifle in the way. The Mauser stock tore through the rifle and collapsed the Sanheel's chest with a wet smack.

His mind seemed to detach from his body as he dropped the weapon and grabbed a Sanheel by the shoulders. He bashed his helm into its face, crushing features into a bloody pulp. Flinging the corpse aside, he saw a pair fleeing into the woods.

A roar bellowed from his speakers, and he started after them, but a blow from behind sent him to the ground, then pinned him down.

"Pull back! Pull back before you redline!" Aignar shouted.

Santos came back into himself, suddenly aware of the alerts flashing through his HUD. The crack of Aignar's gauss cannons hit Santos's receptors and he felt his heart pounding in his chest and skull.

The gauss sounded again. Fainter.

"I…I don't know what happened," he said.

Aignar got off his back and swept his smoking barrels over the pile of Sanheel bodies.

"Happens," he said. "Your body dumps adrenaline and your suit feeds it back to you. Synergy loop."

Getting to his hands and knees, Santos looked over at the ugly pile of dead Sanheel as gauss report sounded through the trees. Aignar glanced at the cannons on his forearm, then back to the mountain.

"Can't be Gideon…" he said. "On your feet, kid. Fight ain't over yet."

Santos picked up his Mauser and followed Aignar toward the sound of the guns. An errant bullet cracked into a tree just ahead of them, gouging out a hunk of wood that broke into splinters.

They came over a rise and saw a single Armor battling against Sanheel in gold-colored armor and wielding massive pikes. The Armor had one arm hanging loose to one side and a pike blade embedded in a thigh.

Aignar jumped onto the slope and opened fire. Santos followed, his HUD blinking as it tried to identify the other suit.

The golden Sanheel swung its pike at the third Armor from behind, striking the helm and sending the suit pitching forward.

"Get their attention," Aignar said as he leaned back and fired his Mauser. The round struck beneath a Sanheel and sent up a spray of dirt.

Santos tried to line up a shot, but the strain on his weapon systems of keeping his balance and computing a shot sent a spike of pain into his temples.

He grimaced and slid onto level ground, stumbling like a drunk into a Sanheel, and the two went down in a tangle of limbs.

The Sanheel shoved Santos away and got to its feet first. It reared up and struck two dents into Santos's breastplate, then pulled up again, its spike-tipped hooves glinting in the moon light.

Armor tackled it from the side. The third suit drove a punch spike beneath the alien's jaw and into its brainpan.

"The Risen!" A strangely accented voice came from his rescuer. "There!" The Armor pointed to a Sanheel in gold armor and double red sashes over its torso galloping away.

Aignar put a Mauser round through its back and it pitched forward, sliding through the dirt to a stop.

The new Armor lifted its still-functioning arm toward a dying Sanheel and shot it in the head.

"Who the hell is this?"

"Cha'ril. The kid. Kid. Cha'ril," Aignar said.

"He's awful. How is he still alive?" Cha'ril wrenched the blade from her thigh, looked it over for a second, then tossed it away.

"His sync's all fouled up," Aignar said as he reached behind Santos's helm and connected a data line to a port. "Been a long day for him. You're getting a quick dose of sedatives."

"No, the fight—" Santos tried to bat Aignar's hand away, but a wave of euphoria turned his limbs to jelly. "Oh...wow."

"It'll last a minute. Just enough to take you back into the green...bitch of a headache afterwards. You're welcome," Aignar said.

Santos floated in a chemically induced bliss. He tried to speak, but only a baby-like coo came out.

"That wasn't the Risen," Cha'ril said. "There was no electromagnetic shock of a death transmission. These are the honor guard..."

"Kid said the Risen dismounted. Maybe the target is still in a tank?" Aignar asked.

"Gideon and I destroyed them all with rail fire," she said.

"So that was *you*." Aignar slapped a fresh magazine into his Mauser. "Wait...why are you here? Aren't you supposed to be on maternity leave?"

"The egg is in a crèche. My duty is here," she said.

"What? Just like that? At least tell me if it's a boy or girl," Aignar said.

"Now is not the time...and I don't know. We're keeping it a

surprise," she said.

Pressure built in Santos's skull, like his suit was slowly crushing it between its thumb and forefinger.

"Like a hangover I didn't earn," he said and got to his feet.

"Who's with you?" Aignar asked.

"No one. I came down inside a supply pod. The pod intelligence was certain I would land nearest to the Risen and you all," she said.

"Gideon worked out the logistics—"

"Which I told those secret squires," Cha'ril said. "Those rear echelon mouse fluffers. But General Kendall would only approve my arrival if I came down and immediately linked up with you. When you weren't there, I figured you were reading an ambush right where I thought you'd be."

"You could have told us," Santos said. "Instead, we had to jump through our fourth point of contact to make the attack work."

"Gideon knew exactly what was happening the instant I opened fire," she snapped. "His grasp of tactics exceeds my own, thank you very much."

"Go easy on him. He's new." Aignar nudged Santos's elbow. "We need to track down the real Risen…maybe he stayed at the depot?"

"I heard them talking," Santos said. "He's out here somewhere."

A whine rose in his receptors. He tapped the side of his helm, but the sound grew louder.

"Cut your feeds! Cut them!" Aignar said, beating the heels of his hands against his head.

Santos triggered the emergency disconnect to his suit, and the silence of the pod closed on him. He could still see, but the world beyond was muted. He got Aignar's attention, then touched a phantom watch on his wrist and raised his hands.

Aignar shrugged.

Cha'ril poked him in the chest then touched her antennae. She wanted him to reconnect.

Santos hesitated, then remembered that he was the junior lancer. He was the first to take optional risk, a military tradition from the time men carried bronze weapons into battle.

He activated a single audio receptor and a ululating whine

stung his ear but faded away seconds later. He turned his entire sensor suite back on and gave a double thumbs-up to his lance mates.

"That was weird," he said.

"Send us a playback," Cha'ril said. "Yes…that's a Risen transmission."

"Iron Dragoons," Gideon sent over IR as he appeared at the top of the rise, a Sanheel head gripped by the hair in one hand. *"We are victorious."*

"And there it is." Aignar's helm shook slightly.

Gideon came down the slope quickly. He tossed the head to Aignar and looked over Cha'ril's damage.

"Cha'ril sent video when she made contact with the honor guard," Gideon said. "Three broke away while the fight began."

"Honor guard wouldn't abandon the Risen," she said. "But they would fight long enough for him to get away."

"The remaining Sanheel have scattered." Gideon took the Risen's head back from Aignar and used its hair to tie it into a hydraulic in his neck. It hung from his chest like a barbarian's trophy. "No air extraction. We head north. Link up with III Corps' attack. Intelligence might be able to reverse engineer the Risen's brain implants. Get us another way to track them."

"All the Kesaht the Risen left behind are still there," Santos said.

"That a problem?" Gideon asked.

"No, sir...always ready."

Gideon's legs hinged at the hips and treads came out of housings.

Santos transformed into his travel configuration and the Iron Dragoons rolled out of the battlefield.

Chapter 22

Bullets stitched across the dirt as Ranger Mark Hoss sprinted through a blasted killing field. He panted beneath his skull-shaped visor, his eyes catching dead men and women lying amongst Rakka and the larger Sanheel.

He slid forward and into a trench line, landing hard against a reinforced wall amidst shouts from Rangers. One swung a gauss rifle toward him in confusion.

Hoss slapped it away and added a string of expletives for good measure.

"Lieutenant! Where's the lieutenant?" he shouted.

"Getting ready to launch the assault," a sergeant said.

"Why?"

"Stop him! It's called off." Hoss got up and made his way

through the trench. Rangers knelt against the forward edge as Kesaht fire snapped overhead. Rounds struck the lip of the trench, kicking up small geysers of dirt and whacking into the back wall.

"Lieutenant!" Hoss stepped around a medic tending to a gut-shot soldier.

The Rakka had dug these trenches out by hand, but Rangers had paid for them in blood.

A hand reached out of a bunker and yanked Hoss inside. A single diamond on the Ranger's forehead and shoulder sent a spike of fear into Hoss' chest.

"You trying to get our lieutenant killed?" The first sergeant gave Hoss a rough shake.

"Sorry, Top," Hoss said. "Command post says to cancel the assault."

A helmetless woman in the back of the bunker looked up from a holo display. Her eyes were tired from days without rest—every Ranger on Umbra shared the same look.

"We go over the top in five minutes," the lieutenant said. "Word couldn't have come sooner?"

"Sorry, ma'am," Hoss said. "Comms are shot. Another

runner came out ten minutes ago…guess he got tagged on the way. Send up a blue star cluster so battalion knows you got the word."

"The Kesaht have their backs to the wall." She put on her helmet and slapped her visor down. Her skull face had a green hue for command. "If we don't push now, they'll recover. I do not want to fall back from this trench and take it a third time."

"Reinforcements are coming," Hoss said. "That's all they told me."

"Hooray friction," the lieutenant deadpanned as she drew a cylinder with a blue band from her back.

"If the rest of the line goes over the top without us, it'll be a slaughter," the first sergeant said.

"My faith in the chain of command is frayed," the lieutenant said before stepping out of the bunker and slapping the base of the cylinder. There was a pop and blue starbursts shot high into the air. "But it's still there."

"Incoming!" echoed down the line.

"On the wall." The first sergeant pushed Hoss out and onto a firing stoop. Gauss fire snapped as Rangers opened fire. Hoss swung his rifle off the mag locks on his back and slid the barrel over the parapet, careful not to flag his position by waving his barrel in the air.

Rakka ran through No Man's Land between the trench lines. They came in ones and twos, not the mass of screaming bodies he'd fought through before. Rangers cut them down methodically. Not a single Rakka made it to their lines.

A shadow rose out of the smoke, a target Hoss was sure was a Sanheel. He fired a shot and saw a spark from the hit.

He felt tension on the carry handle across the top of his shoulder a split second before the first sergeant yanked him off his feet. Hoss landed hard, and every Ranger on the wall turned and looked at him.

"Check your target." The first sergeant leveled a knife hand at Hoss' chest, and he felt a sense of dread worse than any charging Rakka.

"What'd I do?" Hoss asked.

Gauss fire ceased, and a strange silence fell across the trench.

A giant appeared in the night sky. A Sanheel head swung from its chest.

Rangers fell to one knee and crossed themselves.

"Ferrum corde." The lieutenant brushed the back of her knuckles across her skull's lipless mouth and reached for Gideon's foot.

"Stop," came from the Armor's speakers. "Kallen isn't…" The speakers cut off with a click.

Hoss scrambled to his feet and swallowed hard.

"I am not of the faith." Gideon stepped over the trench and continued through the silent battlefield. Three more suits followed in silence.

"I never…" Hoss flipped his visor up to see the Armor clearly. "I've never seen one so close."

"They real enough for you now?" the first sergeant asked.

Hoss wiped a tear away. "Saint preserved us," he said, daring a quick look to the now-silent enemy lines.

Chapter 23

Santos scrubbed a towel against his short hair. The taste of amniosis was still on his lips, a sensation he only ever noticed when he first came out of his suit. He pulled the towel down the front of his face and looked up at his Armor next to him on the catwalk. There were significantly more dents and gouges across the surface.

He touched his side, matching where the Kesaht shell had hit him, and half expected to feel a bruise, but nothing felt amiss.

"Hey, Mr. Santos," a tech called from down below, next to his Armor's feet.

Santos leaned over the side. The tech tossed something up into the air and Santos caught it: a dirt-caked Bahia knot.

"*Parabens.*" The tech gave him a quick salute and went back to the open panel on the Armor's shin.

"Huh," Santos said and pocketed the knot. He'd nearly forgotten about the prayer for strength and passion the techs had made for him. Whether or not it had been truly answered was a matter of faith he wasn't ready to answer.

He was used to a degree of deference from non-Armor servicemen, which he always attributed to his warrant officer rank. But when he saw how the Rangers reacted to their arrival…he'd heard rumors about Armor being connected to Saint Kallen, but nothing like that.

There was a tap on his shoulder and he turned, coming chin to beak with Cha'ril. Her head quills rustled.

He backpedaled and bumped into the railing.

"Sorry! Sorry, Ms. Cha'ril. Ma'am. Chief?" He half smiled.

"Does your sister know you're here?" she asked with a click.

"Mother!" Aignar called out from his Armor, where he was snapping his legs into their cybernetics.

"That makes more sense," she said. "Maternal instincts would cause distress when a hatchling is in harm's way."

"Mom knows I'm Armor," Santos said, rolling his eyes.

"You were in your pod for what, three days?" She ran a

blunt claw tip down her beak. "A few more weeks and you might have to depilate."

"Shave! Come *on*!" Aignar shouted.

"Did he put you up to this?" Santos asked.

"I understand we save our feces for you," she said. "Human military customs are very strange."

"Give him shit," Aignar said, stomping over as he clicked a mechanical hand and forearm onto an elbow. "Figuratively, my girl. Figuratively."

"What about carbonated beverages all over his personage?" she asked.

"Not in a war zone." Aignar adjusted his fake jaw, stretching the plastic skin from side to side.

"Happy to be here," Santos huffed.

Boots steps approached from behind. A stern-eyed man with three scars down the side of his face stopped next to them and put his hands on his hips.

"Nine hours," Gideon said. "Nine hours until the weather clears and we're back in the fight. Sleep. Maintenance. Cha'ril, you're medically checked out for more time in the pod?"

"My body has recovered fully," she said. "I do not suffer as a female mammal would. So inefficient."

"Where we heading, sir?" Aignar asked.

"Wherever the fighting is hardest," Gideon answered. "The Kesaht broke on three different fronts. We run them down, then we can move to another theater. The general called me up. Cha'ril, see to it we're ready to step off on time."

Gideon locked eyes with Santos. The young Armor stiffened up as the captain seemed to be examining him down to his soul. Finally, Gideon gave him a slight nod and turned away.

"You want to go back on maternity leave?" Aignar asked.

"Why? Look how much trouble you all got into without me," she said. "Aignar, what happened on Mars? What happened with Roland?"

Santos felt a sudden chill.

"Kid…" Aignar's thumb snapped up and he jerked it toward the cemetery door. "You earned a trip to the chow hall for a tray of something hot. Beat it."

"Roger." Santos hurried away, leaving his lance mates to speak privately.

****

"Roland left Gideon alive?" Cha'ril shook her head, her quills swaying.

"Disabled his suit. I can't say I'm surprised." Aignar tapped the back of a metal hand against the railing. "Roland's not a fanatic. He never struck me as one. I don't think he's completely sold on the Ibarras, but we—the Union—forced his hand. Put him on trial for a bogus treason charge? Everyone on Balmaseda was fighting beside the Ibarras. Throw all the Templar in the same jail with him…it's not hard to understand why he turned traitor."

"You agree with Roland?"

"No. No, he's still wrong. Justice delayed is never justice denied. The issue with the Ibarras might…might have been resolved. Prisoner exchange. Who knows? Then the government got serious about the Omega Provision…God. That."

"The Council of Firsts has forbidden any Dotari from participating in such…activities. We are also not to prevent the Union from carrying out orders," she said.

"And what're your feelings?"

"My feelings don't matter. I have my orders."

"Smart answer." Aignar's brows furrowed.

"You think you'll have to put down any illegal Ibarrans? Such a thing would be difficult for me."

"I think we've got enough Kesaht to kill first. Then Vishrakath. Then Naroosha. Then any other alien scum that needs to learn a lesson from the barrel of a gun," Aignar said. "If we're fighting Ibarrans before all of that's resolved, we're wrong."

"Gideon feels that way as well?"

"Nope." Aignar shook his head. "The captain's not in the right mind about this. You understand? There a word in Dotari for 'vendetta'?"

Cha'ril's head canted from side to side and she tapped at the screen on her forearm.

"There are old tales from before my people left our home world," she said. "Such things fell out of our culture during the long journey to Takeni. Small ships are no place for a grudge."

"It's best we never mention Roland ever again," Aignar said. "And hope we never cross swords. He's our enemy now."

"You're sure of this?"

"My feelings don't matter. I have my orders," he said.

"A cheap answer. What of the hatchling? He has not impressed me."

"He has his moments. You know his dad's famous?"

"For what?"

"Alcohol and having lots of illegitimate children. More for the alcohol." Aignar pulled his shoulders back and took a deep breath through his nose.

"That makes you famous?" Cha'ril asked, sidling up to Aignar, pressing her shoulder to his.

"You'd be amazed at what makes humans famous. You don't even have to be good at something. You can just be terrible—but passionate about what you're terrible at—and famous. You ever seen a 21st Century classic film about a man named Johnny and his future wife Lisa?"

"Perhaps later. You know where I can get some coffee beans?" she asked.

"There's instant in the mess hall."

Cha'ril spat on the catwalk.

"I missed you too, Cha'ril."

****

Santos lay on his bunk atop the tightly made sheets. The ring of his plugs felt hot against his skin, nagging him to abandon something as trivial as sleep and return to his suit.

Sighing, he removed a slate from a thigh pocket, swiped it on, and tapped a message. A screen opened and his father sat on a couch.

Orozco wore slacks and a shirt unbuttoned halfway down his chest. He looked like he'd just finished filming another whiskey commercial.

"*Nino*," he said, bringing his hands level with his shoulders and letting them drop to his side. "You made it…Armor. Big shoes to fill, yes? Sorry I couldn't make it to your graduation on Knox—scheduling conflicts. You understand."

Santos smirked. "Busy schedule" was always the excuse.

Orozco's shoulders drooped.

"I blame myself," he said. "I was never around while you

were growing up. And when you came up on your mandatory enlistment…what did I do? I put my foot down. Told you what *not* to do. What an idiot I am. I never told you why the Armor get that reaction from me. I don't like talking about that day. When Elias and the rest held off the Xaros, I was right there. In the middle of it all…it was terrifying. To see the Xaros up close like that, the true Xaros, not their drones…men shouldn't see true evil. It brought out something in me. Something I've not been able to shake. I got over it by—no, I hid it. I hid it with women and work."

Orozco picked up a whiskey glass and held it up with his trademark half smile.

"So, you going the tin-can route—" Orozco looked over a shoulder. "Don't tell anyone I said that. You going to the Armor Corps brought back a host of issues. Excuse? Yeah. Good one. No. So what, huh? This just your old man trying to justify being a bum? Maybe. Probably."

Orozco set the glass down and slid it a few inches across the table.

"Stay safe, son," he said and crossed his arms over his chest. "For me. When you come back to Earth, maybe we can go to

Armor Square and I can tell you more of what happened that day. Recording off."

Santos put the slate back into his pocket. He swung his legs over the side of the bed and sat for a few moments, elbows on his knees.

"Now he cares," he muttered. "And he only cares about how it makes him feel."

He got up, re-tucked his sheets to remove wrinkles from his presence, and headed back to the cemetery. He would sleep in his suit, ready for the next call to fight.

Chapter 24

The Templar and Nisei lances marched down a wide ramp to a landing pad on top of a Navarre skyscraper, Marc lagging a few steps behind. The overcast sky held dark clouds, on the verge of rain, though light shone through the thinner areas, creating a dichotomy of doom and hope.

Stacey Ibarra waited on the pad, a squad of bodyguards lined up behind her. Her face was as inscrutable as ever, her silver body covered by a heat cloak to keep the icy effects of her body from freezing those around her.

Colonel Martel knelt to one knee before her. He dipped his head then raised it slowly, taking his hilt off his leg and unsnapping the blade over his knee.

Neither Lady Ibarra nor her bodyguard flinched.

Martel gripped the blade with both hands and raised it over his head. Then, with all the force his Armor could muster, he slammed it toward his knee.

Stacey caught the blade before it could hit home. "Why?" she asked.

"I have failed you, my Lady," Martel said.

The rest of the Armor sank to a knee.

"The Aeon lives?" Stacey asked, her words lilting across the scene.

"She was alive the last we saw her," Martel said.

"Then you have not failed." Stacey plucked the sword out of the colonel's grasp. The weapon looked almost unwieldy in her hand, but she tossed it up slightly and caught it by the hilt. The blade retracted into the guard.

"Grandfather?" she asked.

Marc came forward and handed her Trinia's necklace. The data crystals glowed with an inner light and she rubbed a thumb across the central jewel.

"The Aeon gave us what we need for a final victory," Stacey said. "I declare her part of the Ibarra Nation. Does the Nation abandon their own?"

"Never, my Lady," Martel said.

"Then she will be free. What say you, Templar?"

"By my honor and my Armor," Martel said and beat a fist against his heart as the rest of the Armor repeated the oath.

Stacey handed the hilt back to Martel. "Preparations must be made," she said. "I will summon you when I am ready." She turned and gestured for Marc to follow her and the two immortals left, flanked by bodyguards.

Martel waited until they'd disappeared through a doorway before rising. Big drops of rain smacked against his helm then a downpour engulfed the Armor.

"Templar," he said, "leave your suits in the cemetery then report to the dojo. We train until morning. We will never be found wanting again."

Roland punched the tarmac and cracks opened around the impact.

Chapter 25

Roland stripped off his uniform top, his cramped muscles almost failing as he removed the sweat-logged coat from his shoulders. His quarters were unintentionally Spartan. He'd slept in it a handful of times and hadn't bothered to do anything with the space other than hang up his issued clothing. He took a moment between breaths before reaching into his closet.

Training had been intense. Sword work followed by the VR range in Armor until the targeting computers had recalibrated, then back to the mats. He'd not sparred with the Nisei before, and he learned a number of Iado and Kendo strikes the hard way.

A knock at his door kicked his heart into overdrive and he lunged for his uniform gauntlet he'd left on a small, two-person table. He feared he'd missed an alert or summons from Colonel

Martel, but there was nothing in his message queue.

He limped over to the door, a welt in his thigh tightening his gait. Opening the door, he got a glimpse of void-black hair as Makarov rushed inside.

"Close it, close it," she hissed.

Immediately conscious of his body order and disheveled appearance, Roland frowned and hit a button to slide the door shut. Makarov, wearing simple overalls that bore no rank or unit patches, set a padded bag on the small table.

"I was…" He jerked a thumb to the shower then went red in the face. "I mean, I was—"

"You look like you were beaten with a stick." She sat at the table and pulled a clip out of her hair, letting curls spill out across her shoulders.

Roland swallowed hard, unable to find words.

"I've heard Armor training is intense. Who gave you that one?" she asked, brushing a light finger across his cheek.

Roland touched the spot and winched. "I think it was Morrigan," he said. "Save someone's life and they don't take it easy on you when it's time to grapple."

Makarov opened a flap on the bag and pulled out a cardboard carton, the smell of tomato sauce and spices wafting out.

"I know a guy," she said. "Works the hydroponics farms and makes these by request."

"Do admirals have trouble getting pizza?" Roland's mouth watered as she opened the box—pepperoni, the standard by which all pies are judged.

"Can't pull rank for this sort of thing," she said. "I went in mufti and told him it was for the Black Knight," she said. "You have a couple autographs to sign. I think I could have got some Italian sausage toppings out of him."

She half lifted a slice out, then looked at the empty seat. "It'll get cold," she said.

"I stink on ice," Roland said, glancing back at the shower.

"It'll get cold," she repeated.

Roland sat, feeling a number of new bruises he hadn't been aware of until then. He reached into the box, practically tasting it, when he caught himself. Bowing his head, he said a quick prayer, thanking God and Fate for a meal he didn't even know was possible.

He looked up just as Makarov crossed herself.

"*Za zdorovja*," she said and touched her slice to his in cheers.

Roland took a bite, and the taste brought him back to happier, easier times. They wolfed down the first slice and Roland dabbed at his lips with a napkin. When he pulled it back, he was unsure if the red was tomato sauce or blood from a split lip.

Makarov stifled a laugh. "I'm sorry," she said, covering her mouth, "but how does the other guy look?"

"Based on the number of licks I got in? Probably a hell of a lot better," he said.

She giggled, ending with a snort, and then looked around his quarters. "So…this is what it feels like to be normal?" she asked.

"There was a time when I was a broke busboy in Phoenix," he said, feeling the weight of the plugs at the base of his skull. "That was normal enough. This…is special."

"I have a briefing in half an hour," she said. "And if you think I'm leaving any of this behind…you are wrong."

"Challenge accepted." He reached for a slice across from him and she slapped his hand away.

"You think…" she paused and looked up at him, "you think

things will ever be 'normal'?"

"Not if we lose this fight."

"Then it's up to us to win." She raised an eyebrow at him and kept eating.

Chapter 26

Toth hands grabbed Trinia by the arms and she felt the warm air of a warrior's breath through the hood over her face. A claw poked against the bare flesh of her arms, goading her to get on her feet and start walking. Any hesitation would draw blood.

She'd learned a good deal about the Toth since they took her prisoner. Cruelty was their only way to communicate with her.

In darkness, she went down a ramp and was manhandled onto a seat too small for her frame. She heard Toth warriors barking commands and a sibilant hiss of several creatures in reply.

I'm out of the ship, at least, she thought as stale air wafted through the hood. The dreadnought smelt of moss and old oil. This was someplace different.

Her seat lurched as the transportation she was in moved

forward. The warrior's grip shifted to the back of her neck as the clamp of air-lock doors sounded behind her.

The transport slowed and the Toth shoved her to one side. She landed hard, rolling to a stop when her hip hit something metal. She heard the whine of hydraulics and the whirl of gears and her hood was plucked away.

A clawed metal leg was just in front of her face, the talons inlaid with gold and ivory.

"Be afraid," said Overlord Bale as his tank arms grabbed Trinia by the wrist and hoisted her into the air.

The Aeon was brought level with the brain floating inside the tank. Tendrils touched the inside of the glass, as though it wanted to caress her.

"The last of all the Aeon," Bale said. "What a prize you would have been."

Trinia saw her reflection in the glass. Her eyes were worn, and her face carried the sorrow of failure.

"Get it over with," she spat.

Bale dropped her to the ground and a leg clamped down around her throat. Trinia gasped as Bale jerked her in front of his tank and a platinum spike emerged from the housing just beneath his tank. The spike snapped open, and tiny feeder tendrils stretched toward her.

"Once...once you would have been a great meal of memory," the overlord said. "A treat to be envied, an experience to be savored...just a taste, perhaps?"

A single tendril brushed against her forehead and Trinia closed her eyes.

The spike shut and Trinia was thrown to the ground.

"But things have changed, haven't they?" Bale asked. "I am the last of my caste. The last of the overlords that would have had dominion over the galaxy had the humans not...outplayed us."

Trinia looked around, searching for an exit. A single observation wall overlooked a desert planet and behind her was a door guarded by two Toth warriors in crystal armor.

"You brought it on yourself," Trinia said, wiping a hand across her mouth and eyeing the halberds the warriors held. "I remember when Mentiq tried to kidnap a Qa'Resh, how that almost destroyed the Alliance."

"Mentiq had his proclivities," Bale said, "his

peculiarities...his tastes. It was his appetite that destroyed him in the end. That was your doing, yes?"

"I helped," Trinia said.

"And was it you that brought Malal to my world and murdered billions of Toth?"

"No. Though I would have liked to see it happen with my own eyes. The galaxy is a better place with the Toth gone...you must be the last of the stain." She stood up and raised her chin slightly.

"Trying to antagonize me into harming you?" Bale scratched at the deck with his forelegs. "Curious...you gave yourself up so easily on your empty world. You were an easy transport. Most meat species fight hard during transit. You've either embraced your fate...or you're clinging to hope. Interesting."

"And why haven't you consumed my mind?" she asked, her hand passing over her shoulder. "Swallowed my soul."

"Why, indeed." Bale moved to one side of the observation room and a panel lit up. The muffled sound of moving machinery came through the wall. "You are a scientist, though perhaps not one versed in my glorious state of being. Consuming neural energy is a...method of pleasure. Not a method for education. Feasting on you would bring me days of euphoria...and a few of your surface thoughts. Gain a drop in the ocean that is your millennia of experience? A waste. You are a jewel beyond price, not one I will shatter just to see the cracks."

"Then why am I alive?" she asked.

"The work! The work, of course," Bale said, stepping back as a panel opened in the wall and a tube larger than Bale's tank emerged, filled with light-green fluid. A humanoid shape floated within.

Lights flickered along the base of Bale's housing.

A misshapen human thumped against the glass, features twisted, eyes dead but locked open. A bubble shot from his mouth and crawled up his face.

Trinia recoiled, but Bale grabbed her by the wrist before she could get more than a step away.

"To destroy your enemy's cities is the lowest form of victory," the Toth said. "Burn the worlds? Drive them into extinction? Better, but not exquisite. To enslave the enemy. To feast on their children for centuries until the race knows nothing but despair and devolves into little better than livestock…that is what it means to triumph.

"Humans achieved a victory, that's true. But *I*, Bale, will prove to the galaxy what it is to fight the Toth. I will destroy Earth. The Ibarra worlds. Ignite every sky where they draw breath…then I will sip their minds, feast on their sorrow, until I can raise more overlords and punish the humans until the last star burns away."

"They beat the Xaros," Trinia said. "They can beat you and your Kesaht servants."

"Different wars require different tactics," Bale said. "And I have a number of other races that share my desired ends for humanity. This time will be different."

Trinia pulled her hand free from Bale's claws and regarded the misshapen mass in the tank.

"You've tried to re-create the procedurals, haven't you? You're a butcher, Toth. Not an artisan."

"Setbacks, yes." Bale's tendrils quivered with annoyance. "Is that why the Ibarras wanted you? A kink in their production line? Something only the originator could fix? Irrelevant. Now that you're here, your talents will be put to proper use."

"I will never help you." She gave him an evil look.

"But I am so hungry," Bale said.

A hatch opened on the wall and a cage was pushed out onto the floor. A human girl was inside. She looked at Bale and began sobbing.

"What? No—" Trinia started forward, but a Toth warrior grabbed her from behind.

Bale ripped the top of the cage open and the girl began screaming. Bale's claw tip closed around the girl's neck and he slowly—almost gently—lifted her out of the cage as tears streamed down her dirty face.

The feeder spike snapped open and shut as it approached the girl's face.

"They're so tender at this age…" Bale said.

"Stop. Stop!" Trinia struggled against the warrior's grip.

The spike pulled back ever so slightly, the feeder tendrils stretched toward the girl, stopping only a few inches shy of her.

"Empathy…curious," the overlord said. "Is it because your species share a form? Do you look upon this one and see all the Aeon you killed with your mistake? What's the life of this one to you? I have many more."

"Don't hurt her...please." Trinia lowered her chin.

The warrior let her go and she stumbled forward.

Bale tossed the girl toward her. The child landed badly, shrieking in pain as she rolled to a stop, clutching an arm to her side.

Trinia crawled forward and pulled the girl against her, her size making the child appear like a baby cradled in her arms.

"You will complete my garden," Bale said. "Fully grown human minds and bodies. Any delays or sabotage and I will feast on that one before your very eyes. Then I will give you a new whelp to care for. Another mewling calf to pay the price for your failures."

The girl buried her face in Trinia's bosom, sobbing.

"You'll have it," Trinia said. "When can I begin the work?"

"Pity," Bale said, tapping his claws against the deck. "I'm a bit peckish. I'll see you taken to the lab. Updates every orbit of this station. Tarry, and that one will pay the price."

Bale's legs raised the tank up and he left the room.

Brushing hair from the girl's face, Trinia asked, "Your

name?"

"Maggie," the child said as her face scrunched up and another cry roiled to the surface.

"I won't let anything bad happen to you anymore, little one. I promise."

"I'm scared."

"I know. I know." Trinia looked over at the tank containing the mutated procedural. "This is what I do best. You have nothing to worry about. Trust me."

Chapter 27

The doors to Stacey's laboratory slid open as she approached. The room was circular, ringed by stacks atop of stacks of computer banks that stretched so high the upper reaches were lost in haze.

She walked into a semicircle of holo screens in the center of the room and a small dais raised her a few feet into the air.

Marc Ibarra hesitated in the doorway, his gaze on the bottom of the dais where Stacey's flesh-and-blood body lay beneath, still in stasis, held moments away from death. A pair of humorless bodyguards flanked him.

Stacey raised her hands and the holo panels came to life with golden lattices that twisted around each other and made new connections between the nodes: Qa'Resh writing. Power thrummed through the computer banks around them.

She removed a jewel from Trinia's necklace and dropped it onto a panel. An anti-grav field caught it and suspended it in the air. The Qa'Resh writing in the holo panels changed, and alien writing washed over the screens.

"Stacey," Marc said evenly. "We need to talk. Alone."

She waggled two fingers in the air and the bodyguards left, the doors sliding shut with a pneumatic hiss.

"Why?" Marc moved toward the dais, his fists at his chest. "She was your friend. She saved Earth with the procedurals and now—"

"The galaxy is a selfish place, Grandfather." Stacey reached into a holo screen and flipped over a knot of script. It turned into a Qa'Resh lattice for a second before reverting. "Trinia had information I needed. If it came from her directly or from her notes…the notes are better. She might lie to me if she disagreed with our plan. Her written work…no such concerns."

"The Toth have her!" Marc started up the few stairs to the dais and bounced off a force field.

"And that means one of two things," Stacey said. "Bale has

already ended her or they'll put her to work. We can do nothing in the case of the former. The latter offers some hope for her. The overlord is no fool. He knows what she's worth."

"If she makes procedurals for him," Marc said as he began pacing around the dais, hands clasped behind his back, "then he will have an unlimited supply of human beings. Cattle. Slave soldiers. It's a betrayal to our Nation—"

"My Nation." Stacey glared at him through the holo screens. "You're a bystander, Grandfather. You gave up your mantle when you tried to betray us to Earth."

"It's a betrayal to everything the Nation stands for if we let the Toth and Kesaht torture Trinia into cooperating with them," Marc said. "And there's no guarantee everything you need is in those notes. That is the sum total of millennia of work with Qa'Resh technology. You think the crib sheets are exactly what we need?"

"They'll be enough," she replied.

"You don't know that! You want to find the Ark and realize *then* that she has some missing piece?"

"I have work to do and you're becoming a distraction,"

Stacey said. "What do you want?"

"Save her! I saw the reports from our assets on Earth. We know where the Kesaht are hiding. She has to be held there. Join with the Union and—"

"Never!" Stacey slammed her hands onto the holo projectors and leaned over the side to lock eyes with Marc. "The Union can bleed themselves white against the Kesaht. I. Don't. Care. I will not send my children to fight beside them, not when Garret and the Union will murder them for simply existing."

Marc raised his palms to her. "We have a common enemy. The Kesaht want us just as dead. With our combined fleets, we could end that war and bring the rest of the galaxy to the table."

"You are a fool." She leaned back and swiped a new screen into view. "Once we have the Ark, there will be no one to stand in our way. The last intact and fully functioning Qa'Resh ship in the galaxy. A technological quantum leap. You remember what we saw at the dimension gate, where Malal met justice."

"I'd rather not. His screams were…" Marc turned his gaze away. "This Ark belonged to Malal, didn't it? You want to taint ourselves with that evil?"

"Tools are not evil," Stacey said. "Nor am I."

"We need Trinia," Marc said. "What if you're wrong about the Ark? The longer we wait, the more likely it is that Bale will have what he needs from her and then kill her for sport."

"There is one other group of people with similar experience with Qa'Resh technology," she said. "I've my agents working to procure such an expert now. Much easier than fighting through every Kesaht in their home system."

"What? Who?" Marc cocked his head up at her. "No…Stacey, they're peaceful. Let them—"

The holo panels changed to a galactic map. Tens of thousands of points came up, distributed around the core, but a small swath of the galactic southeast had only a few dots. Marc knew what he was looking at—Crucible gates. The Xaros seeded them over habitable worlds or systems with ancient ruins. The area with fewer gates was old Alliance territory and belonged to species that had built gates in the last few decades after the Ember War.

A golden circle appeared in the outer edge of the Perseus Arm. No Crucible gates were within a hundred light-years.

"The Ark is there?" Marc asked. "But that's in the Null

Zone. The Qa'Resh never contacted any species there."

"Every probe they sent vanished," Stacey said. "The Alliance was so focused on the Xaros, it wasn't worth the time or energy to look harder into the region. But that is where we'll find the Ark."

"And what else will we find there?" he asked. "We might be better off leaving well enough alone before traipsing into someplace that does not want to be bothered."

"If we fight this war without the Ark, billions will die," she said. "If we take this risk, lives will be saved—human lives, at least. Are you afraid of the unknown?"

"Earth's war is our war," Marc said. "You're ignoring the battle right outside our door for-for what? A Hail Mary? A superweapon that might not even exist and one there's no guarantee you can even wield. Trinia needs us. The innocent people on Earth and the colonies need us. Don't talk about a mantle of leadership and just turn your back on them when we're needed the most."

"I need the Ark." Stacey looked down at the dais. Down to her body in stasis beneath. "It will all come together, Grandfather. You'll see. Now…I must prepare my army. If there is something in the Null Zone, we'll be ready to fight for the Ark."

"Stacey, my darling, I'm begging you to—"

She snapped her fingers and the bodyguards returned.

"Gentlemen, return him to his cell and see he's given regular updates on the war effort," she said. "I may have need of him once the *Breitenfeld* is ours. Or not. Goodbye, Mr. Ibarra."

Marc shrugged off the grasp of a guard and walked out of the laboratory, his head stooped in defeat.

Stacey raised her hands like a conductor and began weaving through data.

Chapter 28

Keeper stood in the bottom of the Crucible's bowl-shaped command center. Her eyes were closed, but her surface swirled with fractals as tendrils of light danced from her fingertips to the Crucible's basalt-colored floor.

President Garret and General Laran waited nearby. The head of the Terran Union leaned against an unmanned control panel and checked his watch. Laran had her arms crossed over her stomach, her eyes never wavering from Keeper.

"She said she had it," Garret mumbled. "There are a million fires I have to put out right now. Evaccing colonies. Mercury omnium factory production schedules. A photo op to the macro-cannon emplacement near Vesta that made the mass driver kill. A dozen different military funerals I *should* be at, but—"

"Sir," Laran interrupted as she reached behind her head and touched her plugs, "we're better off being here soon as she succeeds, than being millions of miles away when a decision needs to be made."

"You like waiting?" Garret touched his jacket and felt the bottle of pills in a breast pocket.

"You'd think a flag officer and the commander-in-chief would be immune to hurry up and wait…but here we are," she said.

The light faded away from Keeper's fingers, and the Xaros drone in the shape of a woman turned around.

"I found the Kesaht," she said. A ripple went over her shell, erasing the fractal patterns and changing her appearance to a well-built woman with a lined face. She raised a hand and a map of the galaxy appeared between them. A spiderweb of Crucible networks overlaid the map, and Keeper touched a star far from any gate in space, a star never occupied by the Xaros during their long march through the Milky Way.

"Sigma Tau 9-9," Torni said. "Catalogued as a potential habitable system. On the priority list for second-phase settlement.

The plan was to open a one-way wormhole to the system, build a Crucible with robots, and bring in colonists. The Hale Treaty put a stop to that plan. It was easier to settle worlds with their preexisting gates and increase standoff distance from mass driver attack."

"How do you know the Kesaht are there?" Laran asked.

"Data echoes from the Risen's passing," Keeper said. "They set up a number of hops to different Crucibles throughout the galaxy. There must have been some fidelity loss, as data kept leaking through the system to here. But this is where it stopped."

"Within range of the old jump drives before the Qa'Resh disabled them all," Laran said. "Your theory that the Toth jumped to an inhabited system after their home world was…dealt with…checks out."

"Can we slag the planet?" Garret asked. "Drop a few dozen mass drivers of our own on it?"

"New Bastion will lose their minds if we do that," Laran said. "Support for the Vishrakath alliance evaporated after Novis."

"But no one else has come to our side," Garret said. "They can't help any less than they are now."

"Three gates are within offset jump distance." Keeper waggled her fingers and three points appeared on the map near the Kesaht system. "All settled by the Utishan. They're neutral in this war…and have colonies and Crucibles along our galactic south, the only place we're not fighting pitched battles."

"If we show up to borrow their gates for a little artillery practice, we've got another war on our hands," Garret snarled. "So much for that idea."

"I can get a fleet through to the Kesaht system," Keeper said. "There's a cipher embedded in the Risen signature that overrides the lockout. Same one I've felt moving through the network when other Risen have been killed."

"Then why not open the gate and send a mass driver through?" Garret asked. "A warhead with a thousand nukes to glass their whole planet?"

Keeper gestured to the map and the Kesaht's star came up. Tiny smudges of planets appeared.

"We only have artifact light for Sigma Tau 9-9," she said. "Hundreds of years old by the time it was catalogued. Where anything is in the system now is a guess. They may have settled an asteroid belt, moved to a gas giant's moon. We don't know their defenses. We send a mass driver through, we don't even know what to aim for."

"It must be done," General Laran said, "must be done by the Terran Union in person. Nukes are unreliable. The Crucibles can flood any system with a dampening field to stop any fusion or fission warhead from activating."

"Frag the gate?" Garret asked.

"It will repair itself," Keeper said. "That might buy us a few months."

"We have one shot at a surprise attack," Laran said. "Bring them to their knees quickly now and it will cost us less in ships and blood. If we go back after they have months to fortify…"

Garret sighed and leaned toward the blurry image of the Kesaht system.

"How many ships can you send through?" he asked.

"If I can keep the wormhole open…there's no limit," Keeper said. "But if they sabotage the gate themselves, break the link soon as we come through, it gets tougher. I can guarantee several hundred of our capital ships can get through in the initial push. Any more than that and they'll detect the disturbance coming to them."

"That should do it," Garret said. "We're not there for a pinpoint strike. We're there to crush the Kesaht once and for all. Wreck their shipyards. Knock them down to the Stone Age. Seize the Crucible and bring the threat of nuclear destruction. Cut their deployed fleets off and let them die on the vine. We'll end them in one swift stroke."

"That many ships is our entire reserve," Laran said. "If anything goes wrong, other fronts will become untenable."

"You mean we'll lose," Garret huffed. "We're not winning this war, General. You know it and I know it. This is our chance to regain the momentum."

"I'll need my Armor Corps," Laran said. "And 14th Fleet soon as they've finished maneuvers over Venus."

"You'll have them, and the 9th and 12th," Garret said. "We'll feign an offensive to the Syracuse sector. Keep the Kesaht from realizing what we're up to."

"There are risks," Keeper said. "If the fleets go through and the Kesaht damage their wormhole…no reinforcements unless the

Utishan let us through. You could be cut off, General. No way to get word in or out."

"Acceptable." The general tugged the front of her tunic to straighten it out. "There will be no substitute for victory."

"I must ask," Keeper said. "What if we invite the Ibarrans to—"

"No," Garret shook his head. "They're not to be trusted. Not now. Not ever."

A ripple went down Keeper's shell.

"You've a problem with that?" Laran asked.

"No, ma'am." Keeper shook her head. "We can beat the Kesaht on our own."

"Recall the *Breitenfeld* from Syracuse," Garret said. "We'll have Admiral Valdar command the fleets. Good for morale." The president plucked a data slate from his jacket and there was a rattle of pills.

He put the slate to his ear and walked out of the control room.

"I'll need at least thirty-six hours," Laran said. "Recall all forward deployed Armor. My Corps will find the Toth overlord and bring his broken shell back to Mars as a trophy. This will be our victory. Not the Templars'. Not for Kallen."

"Then I wish you Godspeed and good hunting," Keeper said. "Don't deny the Saint. Never hurts to have too much help in your corner."

Laran snorted derisively and left.

Keeper double-checked that her appearance was "normal" and sent a signal to recall the Crucible's bridge crew. She looked up through the viewport in the ceiling to Earth and crossed herself.

"*Sancti spiritus adsit nobis gratia. Kallen, ferrum corde…*"

THE END

The Story continues in FERRUM CORDE, available now!

FROM THE AUTHOR

Richard Fox is the author of The Ember War Saga, and several other military history, thriller and space opera novels.

He lives in fabulous Las Vegas with his incredible wife and two boys, amazing children bent on anarchy.

He graduated from the United States Military Academy (West Point) much to his surprise and spent ten years on active duty in the United States Army. He deployed on two combat tours to Iraq and received the Combat Action Badge, Bronze Star and Presidential Unit Citation.

Sign up for his mailing list over at www.richardfoxauthor.com to stay up to date on new releases and get exclusive Ember War short stories. You can contact him at Richard@richardfoxauthor.com

The Ember War Saga:

1.) The Ember War
2.) The Ruins of Anthalas
3.) Blood of Heroes
4.) Earth Defiant
5.) The Gardens of Nibiru
6.) Battle of the Void
7.) The Siege of Earth
8.) The Crucible
9.) The Xaros Reckoning

Printed in Great Britain
by Amazon